DESERT PAINTBOX

DESERT PAINTBOX

•

Jane McBride Choate

AVALON BOOKS
NEW YORK

© Copyright 1999 by Jane McBride Choate
Library of Congress Catalog Card Number: 99-94440
ISBN 0-8034-9363-0
All rights reserved.
All the characters in this book are fictitious,
and any resemblance to actual persons,
living or dead, is purely coincidental.
Published by Thomas Bouregy & Co., Inc.
401 Lafayette Street, New York, NY 10003

PRINTED IN THE UNITED STATES OF AMERICA
ON ACID-FREE PAPER
BY HADDON CRAFTSMEN, BLOOMSBURG, PENNSYLVANIA

To Robert and Taryn, who are writing their own love story.

Chapter One

Rachel Small Deer hurried through life with the brisk steps of someone trying to keep up with her own energy. That was why she was running late. She'd crowded too much into the day and was now paying for it. But a country vet didn't have any choice.

Pregnancy tests. Colic. Fever. Cuts on the ubiquitous barbwire fencing that crisscrossed the county. A vet's life wasn't boring. Neither was it the romantic picture painted by popular authors. Absently, she rubbed her shoulder where a llama's hoof had caught her last week. Twelve stitches later, she was back on the job. And she wouldn't trade it for the world.

She was in hour seventeen of a day that showed no signs of letting up. The last eight of those hours had been spent helping a cow giving birth the hard way. Breached births were never easy.

"Just a little bit more," she coaxed. "We're almost there."

A mournful bawl caused her to wince in sympathy. Quickly she was guiding the calf from the birth canal. The cow nudged the calf with her nose as Rachel rubbed him down with straw. Instinctively, he found his mother's udder and began sucking. Both animals were doing well.

She left the barn with thanks from the farmer and two home-cured hams as payment. Though the practice of bartering for veterinarian services had virtually disappeared near the turn of the century in most areas, she frequently accepted goods from her clients in place of cash. Many of the people of the impoverished county where she made her home had too many bills to pay for a vet's service and too much pride to accept charity.

She was in no position to criticize. Wasn't that why it had taken her nearly ten years to earn her DVM? She'd refused money from her grandfather when he had offered to help pay for her schooling, preferring to do it on her own. And she was still paying off the debts she'd incurred for her education.

Now she felt drained, wishing for a hamburger and eight hours of sleep. The first she'd grab on her way back to the clinic after the job was completed; the second would remain exactly that. A wish.

A seventeen-hour day wasn't unusual. There were some nights when she fell into bed that she imagined she heard her shoulders and arms weeping with fatigue and her feet begging for mercy.

Vets in other counties worked out a rotating on-call schedule, allowing each to take a vacation or get a full night's rest. Since she was the only vet in the county, Rachel didn't have that luxury.

She ignored the cramp in her neck and the stale smell of clothes too long worn. That those clothes were covered with bits of straw and blood didn't help. She barely noticed the barnyard smells that clung to her, though. They were part and parcel of her chosen profession. A vet who specialized in large animal work couldn't afford a finicky nose.

Still, she'd rather endure a dozen such deliveries than pay her next visit. A call to Erastus Snow's ranch always meant trouble. Erastus was so cheap he'd steal the oink from a pig if he could manage it, and he avoided vet bills whenever he could get away with it. Fines for animal abuse issued by the local sheriff after she'd put a bug in his ear hadn't endeared her to the rancher.

The ride to the Snow ranch was all too familiar. She'd made the same drive too many times before. Each time the outcome was the same. Still she held onto the hope that this time would be different.

Twenty minutes later, her lips flattened into a hard line as she took in the sight before her. A ewe, nearly dead from a bad birthing, had been left to die at the far corner of a filthy outbuilding. Rachel had only learned of it because one of Snow's employees had risked his job by reporting it.

She had cited Snow twice before for neglecting his animals. This latest incident went far beyond simple neglect, though. It was out-and-out cruelty.

Rachel didn't let much rile her. She was practical enough to recognize that a lot of what went on didn't merit official intervention. Mistreating animals wasn't one of them. She'd called the law out on more than one rancher who put dollars over the welfare of his stock. One irate man wasn't going to intimidate her out of doing her job, even if that man held a pitchfork and a grudge.

The night deepened around her, the air chilling as she worked in the drafty building. She pulled her jacket more tightly around her. Her hands turned icy as she labored over the animal. A shudder trembled through her.

Finally, she stood, her body protesting the cold and her own weariness. Out of habit, she ignored her discomfort. She'd seen animals in worse shape, but not many. Most ranchers, when faced with such a situation, had the decency to call her and have her put the sheep down, humanely and quickly. It was kinder than allowing the poor beast to suffer. No vet enjoyed having to euthanize an animal, but they did it out of compassion.

Still, she believed in saving lives when possible. She gave the animal something to help it sleep. Sometimes simple sleep accomplished what all the modern medicines could not.

Hands planted on hips, she glared at Snow. "You were going to let her die, weren't you?" She didn't give him a chance to answer but poked her finger at his chest, causing him to back up a step. "You start taking care of her, or . . ." The rest of the threat went unfinished. She shivered once more, more out of anger than the cold. "And that means you get her into a clean, heated stall. She won't last another night in here."

Just as quickly as the anger appeared, it dissolved. She'd learned years ago that anger didn't solve problems; it created them.

"I got other animals in the barn," he whined.

"Your parlor or your barn. I don't care which." Another glance at the ewe had her fisting her hands at her sides. Deliberately, she unclenched them, forcing herself to relax.

Erastus Snow waved a pitchfork at her. "You think you're all high and mighty now that you've gone to some slick school and got your fancy degree. Well, let me tell you, you're still just reservation trash. Your ma and pa never had two cents to rub together, but they always thought they were better than the rest of us." He gave her shabby coat and worn jeans a disparaging glance. "Looks like you're cut out of the same cloth."

She folded her arms across her chest and counted to ten. Snow was the worst kind of bigot. He hired members of the reservation to work his ranch but treated them like second-class citizens. He dealt with them in business and then complained that they cheated him. He skirted the law close enough and often enough to keep the sheriff constantly looking over his shoulder.

"You have two choices: take care of this ewe or go to jail. Right now, I'm hoping you'll choose the second." She bent to give the ewe a gentle pat. "I'll find a home for her." It wouldn't be the first time she'd taken a sick animal home with her.

Snow fisted beefy hands on his hips. "No one takes my animals. Not without paying for 'em, he don't. Never can tell. It might pull through."

Now she understood. He wouldn't put the ewe down, but neither would he give it the care it needed. If the animal survived, he'd use it for another season or so. If not, he wasn't out the vet's fee to euthanize it. He didn't come by his reputation for penny-pinching for nothing.

Snow blustered and huffed. In the end, when Rachel refused to budge, he nodded in grudging agreement.

She started back to town only after she was satisfied he intended to follow her instructions. Snow had been a pain in the rear for as long as she could remember. He'd given her father the same kind of trouble. It didn't look like things had changed any. She could tolerate his slurs about her and even her heritage, but she wasn't going to let him get away with what she'd seen tonight.

The image of the ewe, suffering pathetically from infection, ate away at Rachel. Tears crowded her eyes, and she swiped at them with an angry gesture. Tears didn't accomplish anything; they only drained her strength. Tomorrow, she intended on having the sheriff serve Snow with a warrant to inspect his barn and the rest of his outbuildings. She wouldn't put it past him to have more animals in need of care hidden away.

Two hours later, after a stop at her clinic where she caught up on the paperwork that seemed to multiply faster than a pair of rabbits, she stumbled into the loft apartment above the clinic and tried to muster the energy to make herself something to eat. She gave it up in favor of pulling off her clothes and standing under the shower. The water pipes sputtered in protest, the hot water all too soon fading to lukewarm, then cold.

Wrapped in a tatty robe, she brewed herself a cup of tea, then sat cross-legged on her bed while she sipped it, trying to forget the exhaustion and discouragement that sat heavily on her shoulders.

The decision to return to her home in Los Cincos, New Mexico, hadn't been an easy one. She'd lived away from the reservation and its people for nearly ten years. She hadn't expected to be welcomed back with open arms, but neither had she expected the hostility she felt from her own people.

They saw her as an outsider, a woman neither white nor Navajo. With her mother's blue eyes and father's dark hair, her looks were a constant reminder of her mixed heritage.

She felt caught between the world of her childhood and the world she had learned to live in during her years away. She'd been gone from Los Cincos for a number of years, but she'd grown up here. She knew the people, how they thought, what they believed. What's more, she genuinely liked them.

There was so much she wanted to teach them, to do for them. And therein lay the problem. They resisted her bringing what they saw as foreign ideas to a culture thousands of years old. She revered the traditions her people held dear; she also knew there were other ways, new ways, that could better their lives. Her own people regarded her with a skeptical tolerance that bordered on distrust.

Finding the balance between tradition and science demanded every ounce of tact and wisdom she possessed. She only hoped she was up to the challenge.

Rachel had no illusions about herself. She had no

great talents. All she had was a heart that some claimed was too soft for her own good.

She preferred to think of it as practical. Seeing the good in people often brought out that same good. But she didn't go around wearing rose-colored glasses. Hers were ground from the harsh reality of growing up on the reservation.

A man—or woman—always had choices, her grandfather was fond of saying. What she did with them was what made the difference. Rachel intended to make her choices count.

Nick Cassavettes looked around the small studio he'd rented in Los Cincos. It was a far cry from the spacious rooms that he'd renovated in a Denver warehouse. These cramped quarters were less than half the size of his permanent studio, but the unbroken expanse of glass stretching across the east and west walls were impossible to resist. An artist relied on brushes and pigments, charcoal and canvas, but light was the greatest tool of all.

Making his dream come true had been a long time in coming, but he'd succeeded. His desire and need to paint had ruled his life for as long as he could remember. When success had come, he'd been ready. Or so he thought. Instead of finding the satisfaction he'd sought, he had become obsessed with his work.

Work and more work had taken over his life until he went home only to shower and change.

Ironically, now that he had no life outside his work, he discovered he couldn't paint. He'd started dozens of canvases, only to toss each aside after a day or so. Ideas, which had once sprung to his mind with ridiculous ease, now remained stubbornly absent. The few pieces he'd managed to finish were flat and uninspired. He'd trashed them, unable to bear looking at them.

He'd come to Los Cincos to search for the joy he'd once found in his art. The move represented more than a change of scenery. He was on a quest to find his way back. He had come here to reclaim what had been his life. He dared not think that he might not succeed.

Los Cincos had changed in the last decade. His research had turned that up. He understood much of the change was due to people like himself—artists drawn to the beauty of the Southwest. He also understood that he'd probably meet with opposition.

Taos had grown too urban, too sophisticated for many of those who flocked to the Southwest. They had then sought out another town, free of the veneer of polish that outsiders inevitably brought.

But nothing remained untouched forever.

His agent, after practically kicking Nick out of Denver, warned him that the natives of the area strongly resented outsiders. He needed a guide. He

Desert Paintbox 11

recognized that he might have difficulty in finding someone willing to help him.

He did a minimum of unpacking. His paints and easels were carefully laid out. The rest could wait. He stepped outside and lifted his face to the sun. Its rays only hinted at the heat that would soon smother the land. For now, it warmed him and cast a pleasant glow over the land.

He stepped outside. Dusk had just announced itself with an array of colors that defied words. Sunsets in the city couldn't touch those that the desert produced. The magnificent scenery of the New Mexico landscape would inspire anyone, even a burned-out artist like himself. Saguaro cactus rose like misshapen fists pointing at the sky. The stark land was crisscrossed by canyons and dry creek beds, ringed by cloud-dusting mountains.

Hope ... and desperation ... turned his footsteps back to the studio.

He arranged his easel to face the west window. It could easily enough be moved to adjust for the east morning light. The stunning canvas painted by nature's hand humbled him. Rose and magenta, violet and lavender merged together to stain the sky in glorious alliance. How could he hope to capture such beauty?

He stared, mesmerized by the sheer grandeur of the panorama stretched before him.

He began by sketching, his fingers awkward, his

hands clumsy and slow. More out of practice than desire, he ignored the great empty place where his soul had once been.

An hour later, he tore the canvas from the easel and threw it to the ground. The decision to move to the Southwest hadn't come easy. Nick might still be floundering if not for his agent. "Get your head on straight," Jerry had said. "Then come back and see me."

Nick didn't blame Jerry. Jerry had been his agent from the beginning, when Nick lived in a two-room dump and didn't have much more to his name than a head full of dreams. Jerry had seen him through the rough times when Nick's only sales had been at craft fairs. When his work had taken off and caught the attention of the right people, Jerry had guided him through the intricacies of the art world and set up showings in Denver galleries. Up until a year ago, Nick had worked steadily, turning out a couple of major pieces every year. Then the accident had happened, killing his brother, Sam. The bottom had dropped out of Nick's world, taking his talent with it.

Each attempt to paint had ended with guilt. And fear that he'd never again find his way back to the art that fed his soul.

Sam. The name still had the power to turn his heart over in his chest and cause tears to sting his eyes.

Sam had always been restless, ready to try anything—except work. When Nick had hit it big with his art, Sam gave up even the pretense of working and had ridden along on the coattails of his big brother's success. And Nick had let him.

Their parents had hovered on the harsh edge of poverty all their lives. They'd loved their kids, but their energies were taken up in the fight for survival.

When their had father died in a mine accident, their mother had drawn into herself, finding solace in memories rather than her children. She'd slipped quietly away within the next year, leaving the boys on their own. With only a dream and a willingness to work, Nick had pulled both himself and Sam out of the one-horse Wyoming oil town.

"Sam's got a wild streak," their mother had said before she died. "He's not steady like you, Nick. You take care of him, you hear?"

And Nick had. He'd gone along with Sam's crazy stunts, including parachuting, bungee jumping, and climbing mountains that they had no business trying to scale. Nick had planned to go along on the last trip until his agent had scheduled a showing at a prestigious San Francisco gallery. He had let Sam go on without him with a promise that Nick would join him for the next climb.

Though both he and Sam had made other successful climbs, Nick had sensed that this one was somehow different, but he'd ignored those feelings, too elated over the opportunity to introduce his work to the West Coast. That would haunt him for the rest of his life.

Sam had ignored the warnings from park rangers about the dangers of climbing alone. An investigation into the accident said that carelessness had caused Sam's fall to the canyon floor.

Nick knew better. He blamed himself. His selfishness had cost his brother his life.

His heart gave the expected hitch, that little hiccup that signaled the pain was still there. He was fiercely glad that it was. Pain meant that he still felt something for Sam. If that vanished, he'd have nothing. And he wasn't prepared for that.

Nick shook off the memories.

Memories weren't something he allowed himself often. They were a luxury. And like his feelings, he rationed them. He feared if he were to expose them too frequently to the harsh light of reality, they would fade so completely that there would be nothing left of them. He couldn't bear that. Even the painful ones were precious because they were all he had left.

A scrabbling sound at the kitchen door had him frowning. Big-city ways died hard. He dropped his charcoal and went to the door to investigate. A pile of bones lay in the doorway. Closer inspection revealed the heap of bones to be a dog. Nick stooped to investigate. The dog looked half starved and was covered with open sores. Heedless of the dirt and blood clinging to the dog's matted fur, he picked the animal up and brought him inside. The dog appeared half-dead. He was just ugly enough to be appealing. Nick had always had a soft place in his heart for the forgotten creatures of the world. His lips flattened in a hard line at the obvious signs of neglect.

A search through his refrigerator revealed a frozen dinner and some milk. Nick set both out. The dog lapped at the milk halfheartedly but seemed too weak to do more than sniff at the food.

Nick gathered the animal up once more and carried it to his truck. He'd spotted a veterinarian's shingle on the outskirts of town. Without wondering why he was bothering with a dog that would probably have to be put down, he headed to the vet's. He pushed the limits of the old truck he'd bought and pulled in at the small building within five minutes.

The wind had kicked up, a harsh slap of heat as he opened the door of his truck and picked up the dog. With his elbow, he rapped on the door.

A woman opened the door. For a moment, he simply stared. She wore faded jeans, a stained shirt, and battered boots. Something that smelled suspiciously like manure clung to her clothes. No makeup enhanced her features; no jewelry softened the rough clothes.

Despite the outward trappings, she was, quite simply, the most beautiful woman he'd ever seen. Dark hair framed a face that might have been conjured out of an artist's fantasies. Deep blue eyes met his squarely. Obviously part Navajo, she reflected the desert itself—gold and blue.

"I need to see the vet." The anger in his voice was directed at himself. For all he knew, the dog could be dying. He had no business staring at this woman, no matter how lovely she was.

"You're looking at her."

He took another look and frowned. She didn't fit in with his image of a vet, a kindly older gentleman in faded corduroy or, perhaps, a young, earnest man wearing a white lab coat.

"Bring him in here," she said, gesturing to a small room with an examination table at its center.

Her reserve vanished quickly as her hands moved over the dog's leg. Whatever doubts Nick might have had faded as he took in the professionalism of her manner. He sensed the gentleness in her hands as she performed the examination.

To distract himself from the worry that gnawed at him, he looked around. The inner office was scrupulously clean, the instruments gleaming.

Anger radiated from her as she lifted her head to meet his gaze. "Some people should never be allowed to have animals."

He couldn't agree more. He was about to say so

when he realized that she thought he was the owner. "He showed up at my door. I brought him here."

She gave him a disbelieving look.

"Hey, it's the truth." He held her gaze until she nodded shortly.

"He's severely malnourished. The wounds look like he's been in some kind of fight. Probably over a scrap of food."

"Is he going to..." Nick couldn't finish the question.

For the first time, she smiled. "I think we can fix him up." She worked quickly, all the while talking to the dog, using her voice to soothe him as she checked him out.

"What about gangrene?"

She took another look at the wounds. "That's a possibility, but I don't think you have to worry about it overmuch." She continued with her work, her tongue caught between her lips as she frowned in concentration. She gave the dog an injection.

"You can take him home in a little while."

"I told you—he's not mine. I can't keep him." Panic crept into his voice. What was he going to do with this pitiful scrap of life? He could barely take care of himself.

She glared at him. "You got something against dogs?"

"It's not that. I just moved here. I don't have time to nursemaid a sick dog."

Her eyes hardened, but her shrug was resigned. "Leave him."

"What will happen to him if I don't keep him?"

"Like you said, it's not your problem."

Nick looked at the dog who stared back at him with sad eyes. It was the acceptance of his fate that reached Nick's heart. "I guess I could keep him ... just for a while. You better give me some instructions."

Her smile beamed approval. "Plenty of rest and good food, and he ought to be all right. Stop by the clinic in a couple of days and I'll take another look at him."

She followed him back to the outer office.

"What do I owe you?" he asked, pulling out his wallet.

She named what seemed a ridiculously low amount. He paid, sparing a moment to look around. He'd always thought you could tell a lot about a person by their surroundings.

The outer office was a small beige room furnished with a utilitarian metal desk, littered with paperwork, two battered file cabinets, and two mismatched chairs. An old-fashioned venetian blind covered the room's only window. A certificate giving the date and school from which she received her degree and a calendar from Lou's Feed and Seed were the only wall art. Obviously, the lady's money went to her practice, not to the decor.

An hour later, Nick settled the dog in a corner of the studio. "You're going to be fine."

The vet had done a good job. Even more, she actually cared. He recognized that in the way she'd treated the dog's injuries, her touch firm but gentle. She had a way with her, he admitted.

He'd appreciated the honesty of her response when he'd asked about the possibility of gangrene. It had taken courage to tell him the truth. Courage was something he admired.

His encounter with Dr. Rachel Small Deer had sparked something within him. When she'd offered him her hand, he'd nearly lost it. Her touch had set off sparks that still had him reeling.

He wanted to chalk it up to exhaustion. But he knew it was more basic than that. He was attracted to her. Heck, attraction didn't begin to describe what he'd felt when her hand had closed around his own.

Rachel sterilized the instruments, all the while her mind on the man who had brought in the dog. Obviously, he hadn't wanted to keep the animal. Just as obviously, he cared what happened to it. Because she cared about every creature she treated, she made a mental note to follow up on the dog. And maybe, just maybe, she'd check out the man as well.

Her lips turned up in a wry smile. The man was probably married with two kids. Now he had a dog to complete the picture. She shook her head at her musings. With a fledgling practice to build, she had no time for daydreaming.

She was a woman who appreciated the unexpected. It was a valuable quality in her job, where the days were filled with surprises, good and bad. Sometimes she longed for some kind of normalcy, but she understood herself well enough to know that routine would bore her within minutes.

Emergencies like today's compounded the time crunch that country vets always faced. She scheduled her days with appointments and routine procedures, but it wasn't uncommon that within minutes of starting her day, the schedule crumbled around her. If a mare was having trouble foaling, it couldn't wait. A bad laceration required immediate treatment. That meant clients waiting at the next farm were put off until she could tend to the emergency.

Spring was typically the busiest, with calving and foaling season producing a plethora of offspring. Summers were when horse owners were most active with their animals, frequently resulting in injuries. In the fall, cattle returned to ranches after spending the summer months in the high country. Winters usually brought a reprieve where she caught up on her reading and attending conferences.

A ninety-hour workweek during the summer wasn't unusual. Nor were the sore muscles that came with the work. And she loved every minute of it. From the time she could accompany her father on his rounds, she had known that she wanted to work with animals.

The work was grueling, the hours impossible, and the patients frequently dangerous. She risked being kicked by a horse, pinned by a cow, or spit on by a llama. Her clients frequently paid their bills late, if they paid at all. And she couldn't imagine doing anything else.

Rachel recognized that she had it easy compared to her ancestors. She'd faced prejudice, yes, but she also had opportunities her grandparents and even her parents had only dreamed of. Giving back, both to the land and its people, was why she was here now.

Experience in the outside world had given her an appreciation for the reservation that eighteen years of living there had failed to instill. Reservation living, with its strict traditions and customs, had cramped her when she was younger. Now those same rituals gave her a sense of belonging. She was beginning to understand what had held her parents here, even though they had struggled their entire lives just to make ends meet. They'd left nothing but some debts and a love for her that she never had cause to doubt.

She had come back to the reservation to try to help her people and to do a job. She didn't deceive herself into believing it was altruism that prompted her decision to return to her home. It went deeper than that. Her roots were here. And so was her heart.

Chapter Two

A week later, Fred, named for Nick's grandfather, had established himself as an important—and, Nick was afraid, permanent—part of his life. No one had shown up to claim the dog in response to the notices Nick had posted around the neighborhood.

Fred had insinuated himself into Nick's once-solitary existence with a persistence that he could only admire. Fred was growing on him, he thought. What surprised him was that he, who had never had a pet in his life, was actually growing to like the homely dog.

It wasn't that hard, Nick reflected. Fred was the soul of congeniality. He bounded into a room and pounced on Nick with such affection that he had no choice but to submit to having his face sloppily washed.

Fred had also developed the habit of jumping on a kitchen chair whenever Nick walked into the kitchen.

"Get down," Nick said, pushing Fred off the chair. "Your bowl is over there." He pointed to where a huge plastic dish occupied a place of honor in front of the sink.

Nick had had little luck in finding someone to show him around the area. Natives treated him like a pariah. Again, he thought of the vet who had treated Fred.

Maybe he could persuade her to act as his guide. He'd learned that she knew her way around, was friendly with both people from the reservation and town. It wasn't going to be easy to convince her, he acknowledged. There'd been a determined set to her mouth, a stubborn jut to her chin.

Well, he had his own share of determination. Climbing his way out of the poverty of a small Wyoming oil town hadn't been easy either. But he'd done it. His lips curved into a smile. With a name like Cassavettes, he couldn't afford to be fainthearted.

"Rough day?" Sally Tallchief, Rachel's secretary, asked. She was a quick learner and a hard worker—important qualifications, as far as Rachel was concerned.

Rachel had just returned from making a statement

to the sheriff concerning Snow and the abuse she'd witnessed. The sheriff, Wally Timmons, had no more use for Snow than she did. Because he'd been away on vacation for the last week, she'd had to wait to make her complaint.

Rachel told Sally about the meeting with the sheriff. "Going to cost Snow five hundred dollars in fines," she said, unable to keep the satisfaction from her voice. Fines wouldn't make up for the treatment the ewe had endured, but they might make Snow think twice before abusing another animal. "Old Erastus wasn't too pleased about having to fork over money for a vet bill plus a fine."

"Next time you ought to add a fee for being obnoxious onto his bill," Sally said, a grin stretching across her lips.

An answering smile quirked Rachel's lips upward in appreciation. The smile died as she thought about Erastus Snow's treatment of his animals. The man was as cheap as they came and twice as mean.

Sally's eyes showed her worry. "Snow'll make trouble for you if you're not careful."

"Careful's my middle name," Rachel said lightly.

"He's not one to cross."

Rachel didn't answer but inwardly she agreed with Sally's assessment. Snow *wasn't* one to cross. But neither was she. So let him make what he would of that.

"Have you met the artist who just moved here?" Sally asked. "Best-looking thing this town has seen in years."

Rachel's lip curled. Just what Los Cincos needed, another artist. They flocked here, drawn by tales of the historic Southwest. When Taos became overrun with artists and galleries, tourists and boutiques, they searched out new spots. She recognized the feelings as unfair but was powerless to stop the resentment that washed over her.

"What would Charlie think?" Rachel teased. Charlie and Sally had been dating since junior high.

Sally rolled her eyes. "Just because I'm in love doesn't mean I can't look. And appreciate."

"So what's this artist's name?"

"Nick something."

"Nick Cassavettes? Dark blond hair, brown eyes, and . . ."

"A body to die for," Sally finished for her.

Rachel sighed. Why did the one man who'd stirred any interest in her in months have to be an artist? Nick Cassavettes and others like him were everything that was wrong with her hometown.

Property prices had skyrocketed while the locals struggled just to pay their taxes. How could they, she wondered resentfully, when outsiders had moved in and bought up whole parcels of land, driving up the price of food, clothing, and everything else?

Desert Paintbox 27

She understood her prejudices and accepted them, but her conscience pulled at her. It wasn't like her to condemn without reason. She'd faced prejudice—against her sex, her race, her choice of profession. She prided herself that she was free of the insidious disease. Now she realized that she was as flawed as anyone who judged another without just cause.

When the subject of her thoughts showed up at the clinic, she was unable to keep the scowl from her face.

Unlike many large men, Nick Cassavettes wore his size comfortably, moving with an easy grace as he walked toward her.

"Dr. Small Deer."

"Mr. Cassavettes." It annoyed her how far back she had to tip her head to meet his gaze. At five-foot-nothing, she was accustomed to people towering over her, but this man topped her by a good foot.

Aware that he was subjecting her to the same scrutiny that she had dispensed, she stood still and let him take his time.

A country vet couldn't be fussy about clothes. She favored jeans and tops with scuffed boots tucked inside her pants. Her long hair was pulled back in a ponytail, her face free of makeup. Whatever he thought of her was kept to himself as he let his gaze travel over her.

Her glance at him was full of dismissal. And contempt. She'd seen his type before. Artists lured to the romance of Los Cincos. Thanks to him and others like him, the once-quiet city had turned into something she didn't recognize. While newcomers brought their wealth and expensive tastes, many Native Americans struggled to make a living in the place they'd spent all their lives.

Nick felt himself subjected to a thorough inspection that made no attempt to be anything than what it was. He had the deflating feeling he didn't measure up. Well, what had he expected? He was an outsider, a city boy with city ways.

He could feel her disapproval of him like an icy rain. It rankled. She was condemning him for no other reason than the fact that he was an outsider.

As it had the first time, her beauty hit him square in the gut. Now he looked beyond the perfect features and creamy skin. It was a face that radiated too much strength to be merely pretty, too much grit to be comfortable. Dark blue eyes, resembling the desert sky at evening, met his gaze squarely.

Her clothes were strictly utilitarian, depending upon her for style. He'd never think of denim in the same way again. The thought had a smile tugging at his lips. Heavy boots caked with mud completed the look. Still, she managed to look wholly feminine.

The overall effect slammed into him. Forcibly, he

reminded himself that he hadn't come to Los Cincos to find romance. He had come to find himself.

"I came to offer you a job. I need someone to show me around, introduce me to members of the reservation."

She lifted a shoulder, the gesture clearly one of rejection. "Sorry. Not interested."

"Care to tell me why not? Are you prejudiced against all newcomers?"

That brought a scowl to her face. "No. Only the ones who come here to paint the quaint—" She nearly sneered the word. "—people they find here."

"What's wrong with painting?"

"Nothing. If that's all you do."

"What other crimes am I guilty of?"

She stepped outside and made a sweeping gesture with her hands. "Look around you. Tell me what you see."

Trendy boutiques and bistros lined the street. Galleries rubbed shoulders with exclusive jewelry stores. It was no longer the town that had drawn artists and craftsmen a century ago, but a playground for the rich and idle. Fashionable tourists with deep pockets strolled down the street. It wasn't the local shops that attracted their business, though, but those of the newcomers with their Beverly Hills labels and pricey merchandise.

She sliced through the air with her hand. "What's happened is that people born here, people who've spent their whole lives here, can't afford to live here anymore." Her voice had grown thick as she fought back tears. That was the last thing she wanted.

"Do you always judge people without knowing anything about them?" With that parting shot, he left.

It shamed her. Oh, how it shamed her.

When Jimmy Whitecloud told her that he was going on a vision quest for a month, she didn't know whether to laugh or to cry. Jimmy had been her assistant, helping her with the animal testing, for over six months.

Without him, she could lose the temporary state contract for animal testing. She'd busted her back to get that contract. And without that, she didn't have a chance of staying in business. Her books showed the business was in the black—just barely. Sure, it was easy to say she ought to handle things more professionally, to demand payment in cash instead of hams, but she couldn't turn away people who needed her help.

She needed help. No doubt about it, she couldn't keep her practice without some kind of assistance in the next couple of weeks.

All she needed, Rachel thought with a touch of

irony, was to clone herself. She thought about the life she'd spent most of her adult years training for.

Five years in college, another five in veterinarian school, and she was still regarded as the new kid on the block. She'd grown up on the reservation, had gone to the reservation school with the local kids and buried both her parents here. Yet she was an outcast. Because she had dared to leave the reservation and seek a life on the outside.

She glanced at her desk and groaned. The bills could no longer be ignored. The practice was slowly coming along, but there were still lean times. Not all her customers paid promptly. Some didn't pay at all . . . either in barter or cash. Her cash flow was down to a trickle. If things didn't change, and soon, that flow would be as dry as a desert creek bed. Given enough time, she knew she could make a go of the business. But time was a luxury she didn't have.

There were alternatives. Give up the animals she'd given shelter to. Start demanding payment from those ranchers who were behind on their bills. Neither was acceptable. The animals in her barn had nowhere else to go. Without her care, they'd be put down. And the ranchers needed her help, whether or not they could afford her services.

She drove to the newspaper office and listed the job opening in the classified pages.

A groan escaped her lips as she saw Erastus Snow, a sneer pulling his lips down, approach her. Her last encounter with Snow still burned in her memory. The sheriff had fined him but had refused to lock him up. As far as she was concerned, the man belonged in a cell.

Erastus was spitting fire and venom. "You done stuck your nose into my business one too many times."

"What can I do for you, Mr. Snow?"

"You can keep that busybody nose of yours out of what's mine. What I do on my land is my business and nobody's but mine."

"That's where you're wrong. What you do to your animals is *my* business. And if you think I'll stand by and watch you abuse another innocent animal just to prove how cheap you are, you can think again. There are laws protecting animals from people like you."

"And there are laws to protect law-abiding citizens from do-gooders like you."

She started to walk away when the rancher clamped a hand over her arm. "You and me got some more talking to do."

"I've got nothing to say to you."

"Don't you get all hoity-toity on me. You cost me a passel of money. You and your highfalutin ideas."

Desert Paintbox 33

"You're only digging yourself in deeper."

"I'll have your job for this."

"You wouldn't want it. The pay's lousy."

His face crimsoned while a vein bulged dangerously above his brow.

Rachel attempted to shake off his hand but found his grip vicelike in its strength. "Let go of me," she ordered in a low voice.

"Not till you promise to quit messing in my business," he said, his voice more menacing than ever.

"The lady told you to let go of her arm." A quiet voice surprised both of them.

Rachel looked up to find Nick Cassavettes towering above them. How had he come upon them so silently?

Abruptly Snow freed Rachel's arm. "The lady and I were just having a friendly disagreement. No harm done."

"I'm just making sure it stays that way. All friendly." Nick's inflection wasn't lost on Rachel. Or, she guessed, by Snow, judging by the taut set of his jaw.

Rachel sent Nick a sharp look, her attention caught by the thread of steel in his voice. His eyes were as hard as the polished turquoise her grandfather used in the jewelry he crafted. She gave an involuntary shiver.

Nick shouldered himself between Rachel and

Snow. "I'll see you back to your truck," he said, taking her hand as if it were the most natural thing in the world.

At her truck, she turned on him. "I could have handled him."

"The man outweighs you by at least a hundred pounds. What would you have done if things had gotten rough?"

She lifted her chin, an instinctive response to the censure in his voice. She was grateful for his intention, but she'd been taking care of herself for a long time. His interference only made it appear she was afraid of Snow. Men like Erastus Snow fed on others' fear. The artist hadn't done her any favors.

"Look, I'm sorry," Nick said. "I only wanted to help."

"Your kind of help I don't need."

"It didn't look that way from where I was standing."

Where did he come by all that arrogance? she wondered. Did he have to work at it or did it just come naturally?

He closed the small space between them, his face so near that she could make out the small lines around his mouth. On anyone else she'd have called them smile lines. This man didn't look like he smiled much, if ever.

There were ghosts in his eyes, she thought with

a certainty that startled her. She wasn't given time to ponder on it.

"You're welcome," he said, sarcasm coating his words.

Rachel stared after him as he crossed the street. She didn't like the knowledge that she'd been in the wrong. It grated on her. Still, the man had no business stepping in when no one had asked for his help. That wasn't quite true, the honest part of her acknowledged. He'd waited, ready to help if she needed it. Well, she hadn't.

Rachel liked to believe that she could handle anything, that she was in control of any situation. The encounter that afternoon left her knowing that she was as vulnerable as the next person. Realizing that had pricked her hard-won self-confidence.

She had work to do. And that didn't leave any time for standing around feeling sorry for herself. She'd indulged in her share of pity-parties in the past, and would probably do so again in the future. But not tonight.

A cloud of failure settled over her as she acknowledged that she was at least partially to blame.

She had grown up in a world of common people and the daily struggle of making ends meet, knowing that few things came her way, at least not without a lot of work on her part. She didn't have big dreams, only ordinary ones.

Nick Cassavettes wouldn't understand the struggles and dreams of the people who made their home in this small town where poverty was the norm and hard work didn't equal success. The thought brought a twinge of conscience. She'd met the man only a few times and already she'd judged him and found him guilty. That wasn't like her.

Nick watched as the pint-sized vet drove away, tires spitting gravel and sand. Anger carried him the few steps back to his studio.

When he'd heard the raised voices, he'd reacted. He hadn't thought, hadn't waited. He knew he'd come on too strong, too fast. The lady had been holding her own. He also knew that given the same set of circumstances, he'd do it all over again. Panic had grabbed him by the throat when he'd seen Rachel confront Snow by herself. A man didn't stand by and watch a lady being accosted.

The pretty veterinarian had made it clear she didn't want or need his help.

He'd done some checking on her. It wasn't hard to find people who knew the lady. Some liked her. Others were withholding judgment. What made her tick? he wondered. Did she make a practice of putting herself at risk?

He'd heard the gossip about her. Reservation girl returns home from the big city.

Frustration poured out of him as he recognized

that he had managed to alienate the one person who might have been able to help him.

Good going, Cassavettes, he congratulated himself. *You can get a job in the diplomatic corps when your painting career blows up in your face.*

Maybe he'd have to learn tact. It had never been one of his strengths. His agent had told him often enough in the past that his blunt tongue was going to get him into trouble. Nick had never paid much attention, but he was beginning to think Jerry had been right.

He'd managed to annoy the petite veterinarian. She had let him know in no uncertain terms that he was persona non grata as far as she was concerned.

The irony was that he'd only meant to help. Instead, he'd put his foot into his mouth and then wedged it in further with each word he'd uttered.

Chapter Three

Sally frowned at Rachel, disapproval setting uncomfortably in her normally cheerful face when Rachel finished relating what had happened. "That's not like you."

"What?"

"Making judgments without knowing the facts. Without knowing the man."

Rachel flushed. Sally was right. It *wasn't* like her. She'd reacted instinctively. The pencil she held snapped between her fingers.

"It wouldn't have hurt to listen to him."

Rachel blinked. Sally couldn't have surprised her more if she'd suggested she dye her hair blond.

"You think I ought to give him a chance?"

"I think you need him." Sally gestured to the books. "If you can't do that testing, you're going to be in a bad way."

"If you don't like the way I do things..." Rachel heard the stiffness in her voice and winced. What was there about Nick Cassavettes that set her back up and had her acting completely out of character? Sally deserved better. More than a secretary, she was also a friend. "You're right."

The criticism rankled. The idea that she was guilty left a bad taste in her mouth. She'd endured her share of racism at school because she was half Navajo and half white. She'd been labeled and dismissed. That she'd been desperately poor during those long years hadn't helped her standing with her classmates either. There'd been no wild rebellion, no spurning the university's rules and regulations as other students did. She hadn't had the time. Or the energy. She'd been too busy working.

Crow wasn't one of her favorite dishes, but it looked like she'd be eating it for dinner.

When her grandfather showed up that afternoon with some of his special herb mixture for wounds, she seized upon it as an excuse to visit the artist. She'd bring him some salve for his dog and make an apology as well.

She found the studio easily enough. Nerves fluttered in her stomach as she knocked at the door.

Nick opened it and gestured her inside. His lifted brow had her holding out the salve in explanation. "My grandfather Ray sent this for your dog."

He examined the small pouch of herb mixture. "What do I owe him?"

"Nothing. Around here, we don't keep score."

"I see."

But he didn't. She could see that in his eyes. The ways of the reservation and small towns baffled many.

She looked around. Reluctantly, she approved the spare lines of the furnishings and flood of light. She took a deep breath. "About today . . . we got off to a bad start," she said. "My fault. I was feeling pretty raw about Snow and took it out on you."

"Don't hog all the credit. I tend to come on a bit strong myself." The generosity of his words struck her.

"Still, I was out of line."

"Yeah. You were." A tiny smile broke at the corners of his mouth, robbing the words from the bite they might have otherwise carried.

"I could have handled him," she said. She'd grown up on the reservation, wrestling with the boys and winning more times than not. What she didn't know how to handle was being protected.

She studied Nick and realized he was more disturbed by the incident than she was. Impulsively, she laid a hand on his arm. "Snow didn't hurt me."

"What put his back up?" he asked.

Briefly, Rachel described what she'd found at Snow's ranch. "I gave my report to the sheriff. He laid a hefty fine on Snow. He didn't take kindly to it.'' The memory had her lips curving upward.

A grin settled on Nick's lips. "You must like riling folks."

"I didn't take this job to win any popularity contests."

His grin died to be replaced by a speculative look. "No, I don't suppose you did."

"I appreciated your help," she said quietly. "He took me by surprise. I'm not normally taken off guard."

"I'm sure you're not," he agreed. "But you're a woman all the same. Doesn't that make it tough—in your job?"

She raised a brow. "Get out of the dark ages, Cassavettes."

"You can't deny there're dangers in your job."

"It goes with the territory."

Nick didn't look convinced. "I don't like to think of you coming up against some rancher who's bent out of shape because you were just doing your job."

His obvious concern warmed her but, at the same time, she bristled at the implication that she was unable to take care of herself.

"I'm stronger than I look," she told him.

For a long, humming moment he studied her. "I guess you are at that."

She needed to break the sudden tension. "How's the dog doing?"

"Fred? He's doing great. I think." He looked uncomfortable. "The truth is... I never had a pet before."

Her eyes softened, along with her heart. *Just a bit,* she told herself staunchly. "Not even a goldfish?"

"No." He lowered his gaze, ashamed of the admission. The truth was his family hadn't had the extra money to feed a pet. Sometimes there hadn't been money to feed his brother and him.

As though aware that he was the subject of conversation, Fred wandered into the room at that moment.

"Then it's time you started." She knelt by the dog, hugging him, heedless of the dog hair that clung to her clothes. "Fred." She said it consideringly. "I like it."

Nick wondered what it would feel like to have her arms around his neck, the enthusiasm in her voice directed at him. The stirring of interest within him was as unwelcome as it was unexpected. He had a life to reclaim. He had no time, no energy for a woman, even one as intriguing as Rachel Small Deer.

She stood, drawing his attention to her petite stature. For all her small size, though, she radiated courage and grit. The cut of her chin, the fire in her eyes, all indicated a woman accustomed to fighting for what she wanted... and getting it. He understood that. Respected it.

His gaze met hers. The disturbing awareness that he'd experienced earlier slammed into him again. He hadn't expected to feel such an immediate and compelling attraction.

To his annoyance, he found he couldn't tear his gaze from her. She looked tired. Shadows underscored her eyes, giving her a bruised look that left him feeling uncomfortable.

He studied her further, making no attempt to hide his frank appraisal. Dark hair tumbled around her cheeks. Her pale gold skin stretched tautly over her cheekbones. Eyes so blue to rival the midday sky held a lively intelligence and a trace of impudence that even her obvious exhaustion couldn't hide. Her no-nonsense clothes and pulled-back hair showed a woman committed to her work. Clearly, she was at home with who—and what—she was.

Rachel Small Deer was more than the sum of her parts, he decided. There was an animation in her features that drew the eye, an impulsiveness that probably led her into trouble more often than not.

She fit here. Not just in the way she was dressed. It was in the way she held himself. Confidence, rather than arrogance, he thought, gave her the air of authority that sat comfortably upon those slim shoulders.

It didn't take him long to size her up and decide that he could probably like her.

"Finished?" she asked.

Caught staring, he flushed. "Not yet. Do you mind?"

"If I'd minded, I'd have said so."

Her bluntness was as refreshing as her unpainted face. She could teach him a lot, and he needed her help. After several weeks here, he was still regarded as an outsider. Before he knew what he was going to say, he was voicing his thoughts aloud.

"I've tried introducing myself. It's not like I'm asking for any special favors. I just want to get to know the people, maybe paint some of them."

She studied him, her eyes full of speculation. And patience. He had no trouble reading her thoughts. They were written all over her face, plain for anyone who took the time to read them. She was wary of him. Well, maybe she had a right to be.

"A lot of people resent outsiders. We're fighting for a way of life here."

He watched the fire grow in her eyes, saw the hectic color tinge her cheeks, her dark eyebrows disappear under the thick fringe of bangs as she tried to make him understand her feelings. He understood. But he didn't feel responsible for them. Or the changes that had come to her hometown. He said as much, earning a frown from her. "Change is inevitable."

"That's good," she said. "You come here and turn our lives upside down and then tell me that change is inevitable."

He recognized how pompous his words must have sounded—even worse, how unfeeling. "I'm sorry."

"I think you mean that."

"You think right." He thought furiously, trying to work out something that could benefit them both. "You need help with your testing. I need a guide. Maybe we can do some trading." At her hesitation, he pressed, "You *do* need help, don't you?" At her raised brow, he added, "I read your ad in the paper."

"*Veterinarian* help."

"I helped my grandpa on his farm. Worked with a vet one summer while putting myself through school. I know my way around farm animals, but not pets. But now with Fred, I'm learning."

For a moment, he stepped back in time. His grandfather's ranch, where he'd spent summers as a boy, gave the young Nick a break from the bleak realities of life in a mining town. At his grandfather's small spread, he'd learned how to milk and groom, help with birthings and vaccinations. The work was hard, constant, and bone-grinding. What he hadn't counted on was the sense of pride he'd felt after the day was over.

"I don't think—" she began.

"Afraid?"

That had her chin angling upward. "No way."

"Why don't we try it for a week? If it doesn't work out, there's no hard feelings. Deal?"

"Deal." She stuck out her hand.

He closed his hand over hers. Lightning streaked through him at the brief contact.

Rachel pulled her hand away before his fingers had completely wrapped around hers. She lowered her gaze but not before he caught the flash of awareness that arced between them. He stared, not trusting his own reaction. Sure that he'd imagined the spark, he willed her to look up, wanting to confirm his own perception. But she kept her eyes stubbornly cast downward.

Maybe that was a kind of evidence in itself, he thought, more curious than ever. Why would she refuse to look at him unless she, too, had felt what he had? And if she had, what then? He wasn't looking for romance, didn't have time for it. He had a life to put back together.

"Rachel?"

Reluctantly, it seemed, she raised her head. Waiting, he supposed, for him to say something. What was he supposed to say? *Did you feel it too? Did you know what was going to happen when our fingers touched, when our eyes connected?*

He settled for something more commonplace. "Thanks. For agreeing to help me."

Desert Paintbox

She didn't answer, only looked at him as though he were some slightly strange creature which required thoughtful study. Well, he *felt* pretty strange. This woman was having a peculiar effect on him, and he was pretty sure he didn't like it.

Didn't like it one bit.

Rachel scowled. She didn't know how it had happened. She didn't like him. Didn't want to like him. But she had given her word. There were few enough things a person could count on in this world. She liked to think her word was one of them.

He made it all sound so simple. It wasn't, and she knew it. What he said, though, made sense. She needed help. Only a fool, her grandfather said, refused help when it was offered. And she was no fool.

Before she knew it, she had agreed to show Nick around the reservation and introduce him to the tribal elders. How could she have guessed that an artist would have training working with large animals? When Nick had volunteered the information that he'd worked his way through art school by assisting the local vet, she knew she couldn't dismiss his suggestion that they help each other.

"If you're really serious about this, meet me at the clinic. Monday morning. Seven o'clock."

He nodded, recognizing the gesture for what it was. A peace offering. The thought gave him hope. He'd show her that she was wrong about him. And, in the process, maybe prove something to himself as well.

It was definitely not a match made in heaven, Rachel thought as she waited for him to show up Monday morning. The man had tricked her. If she'd had an inkling of what he had up his sleeve, she'd have run as fast as she could in the other direction.

She was going to regret this. She knew it just as she knew that she had no choice. When he arrived, she reminded herself it was only for a week.

He faced her in relaxed ease, a near-overpowering presence there in the small clinic. "I was hoping you'd show me around."

"You've seen the clinic. If you'd like, you can meet our permanent boarders." She led him to the barn, set a short distance from the clinic. Inside, she opened a stall door to pat an aging mare. "This is Lucy."

Nick reached out to stroke the velvety nose.

When Lucy backed away, Rachel soothed her with a few words. "Come on, Lucy. Show the man you're a lady."

The mare nudged Nick aside to poke her nose in Rachel's pocket. "You looking for this?" she asked, producing an apple. She polished it against her sleeve before holding it out.

Lucy clamped it between huge teeth and chewed.

He saw the obvious affection Rachel had for the

mare. It was but one more side to her, a side he liked very much.

"How long have you had her?"

"Forever. My grandfather took care of her while I was away at school."

It wasn't every woman who'd keep an aging animal on out of sentiment. But then, he was learning, Rachel wasn't like any woman he'd ever known.

A gelding, fifteen hands high, caught his attention. "He's a beauty."

"That he is." With easy familiarity, she patted the horse's flanks. "This is Galahad."

"Galahad? As in King Arthur and the knights of the round table?"

She nodded. "Doesn't he look like a knight?"

Nick nodded. "A black knight. What else do you have in here?"

She showed him. Each had their own story, he learned.

A goat with a missing leg, left outside the clinic. A llama, abandoned because of a bad temper. A potbellied pig that had outgrown the owner's idea of the proper size for a house pet. He didn't try to count the cats that stalked about the barn, heads high and eyes aloof. Or the dogs that made their home on the porch. What amazed him was the harmony that existed between them.

Sure, Rachel was a vet, trained to care for animals. But that alone didn't account for the compatibility she'd achieved between the animals. Hadn't he found some of that same peace when he was in her presence? Was it a kind of magic that she exercised, on man and animal alike?

"Do you adopt every stray you find?" he asked.

She looked at him sharply, as though sensing criticism. What she saw in his eyes apparently reassured her. Her shrug was self-deprecating. "Usually *they* adopt *me*."

She pointed to a mutt that looked like a cross between a beagle and a border collie. "I found him on my porch." Another dog brushed against her leg. "He was tied outside my barn."

Nick began to understand. Unwanted pets and farm animals who had outgrown their usefulness all eventually found their way to Rachel's place.

"It must cost a fortune to feed them all."

Her smile was more grimace than grin. "Yeah. Cat and dog food doesn't come cheap. Neither does feed for the horses and llamas. The owner of the feed and grain store in town's a friend of my grandfather. He gives me a break on the price."

Nick did some quick calculations. Even if she bought the stuff at cost, the monthly bill for food must be astronomical.

"You're a soft touch."

"Yeah." Her tone said she didn't mind the reputation.

The barn was scrupulously clean, the straw fragrant and fresh. It said as much about her as did the sparsely furnished clinic. Both revealed a facet of the woman he was increasingly attracted to.

"Do you ride?" she asked.

"Try me."

Under her watchful eye, he saddled Galahad. Before he could mount the big gelding, Rachel guided his hand to the horse's neck. "Look into his eyes and tell him that you are grateful for the gift he will give you."

"Gift?"

"His loyalty. His heart. They belong to you for this ride. Treat them carefully." She saddled Lucy.

They set an easy pace, enjoying the ride and the magnificent surroundings. Mighty saguaros spiraled upward. Creosote bushes were a dark green, contrasting with the paler ocotillo and mesquite trees. Red sand provided the backdrop for rock formations.

He was sorry to see the time together come to a close and said as much when the ride was over. "Thank you." He pressed her hand, holding it for a moment longer than necessary, and then followed her into the clinic.

Rachel walked inside, more disturbed by his touch than she wanted to admit.

If Sally noticed how flushed her face was, she

was tactful enough not to comment on it. For some reason, Rachel was reluctant to tell her friend of the incident. Usually, she had no secrets from Sally, but this time was the exception.

"Sorry I'm late. I got . . ." She paused for a moment, "Held up. Everything all right?"

Sally rolled her eyes. "Ben Winslow called. Told me we overcharged him and that he wasn't paying any . . ." Her voice trailed off.

Rachel sighed. "I get the picture."

But her mind wasn't on Ben Winslow, a local rancher, and his cheap ways. It was focused on the agreement she'd made with the artist.

Her grandfather would help, she knew. She wasn't as certain about the other members of the reservation. They were bound in tradition, and she respected that. She'd warned Nick that she couldn't guarantee their cooperation. She would make introductions, and he'd have to take it from there.

After seeing to her scheduled patients, Rachel took Nick on a round of testing. She had to hand it to him, she thought a couple of hours later. He handled the animals with an ease that showed both respect and familiarity.

Following the testing, she headed the truck west.

"What's next?" he asked.

She slanted him a smile. "A visit to the reservation."

Secretly, she hoped he'd fail. Wasn't that why she had agreed to introduce him around the reservation? Members of the tribe weren't going to want some artist making them subjects of his paintings.

She couldn't have been more wrong.

With her endorsement, Nick was welcomed to the reservation. Though the older members might not approve of her, they respected her grandfather. Out of regard for him, they would give help whenever asked.

Old women and little children, young men and teenage girls alike greeted Nick enthusiastically, bombarding him with offers to pose.

The look he gave her was comical. Who'd have thought these normally reticent people would be so eager to have faces immortalized on canvas? Rachel shook her head. As much as she thought she knew her friends and family, she realized there was a lot she didn't understand.

Nick met each person in the same easy way. He gave his complete attention to all he met.

When they left the reservation, she checked in with Sally and learned that Cal Jenkins had called and wanted her to check on his sow.

It was late by the time they reached the Jenkins place. The sun was sliding down the horizon, turning the cottony clouds to pink and purple and gold. By unspoken consent, they spared a moment to appreciate the unmatched beauty of a New Mexico sunset.

As they climbed out of the truck, Nick took a

whiff of the air. "Nothing sweeter than the smell of pigs."

Rachel only smiled. "Wait till you meet Janet. She's a darling."

"Janet?"

"Janet's been acting poorly," Cal said, gesturing to the sow that occupied a large pen all by herself. A large man who prided himself on the quality of his stock, Cal Jenkins was one of the few area farmers who called Rachel in to look at his animals at the first sign of a problem.

Nick managed to entice the sow out from her pen so that Rachel could examine her.

The farmer scratched his head. "Never seen Janet take to anyone the way she took to you," he said to Nick.

Neither had Rachel. She'd tried her best to get on the sow's good side during her visits and had failed miserably. That Nick had managed what she'd failed to do both annoyed and amused her.

"Janet's got worms," Rachel said after a brief examination. She pulled a syringe and medicine from her bag.

Nick moved to help her. The accidental brush of his hand against her arm startled her so badly that she nearly dropped the syringe. With more composure than she felt, she completed the inoculation.

Cal Jenkins looked at Nick with respect. "You handled her slicker than bacon grease."

Desert Paintbox 55

Rachel chuckled. Abruptly, the laugh died in her throat. If Cal could accept Nick, why couldn't she?

"Thanks for getting out here so fast," Cal said. He slapped Nick on the shoulder. "Glad to see Rachel got herself some help, what with Jimmy gone and all."

"Why don't you like me?" Nick asked her as they cleaned up.

She passed him the waterless disinfectant and then used it on her own hands. "I don't dislike you," she said carefully.

"That's not the same thing as liking me."

He was right. It wasn't. How could she explain that she had a feeling that time and the small town she remembered were slipping through her fingers and that she blamed Nick and the others like him? She recognized her feelings as unfair, even prejudiced.

"You and the others, you come here with your fancy cars and fancy clothes and look at us like we're some kind of oddity with our quaint ways and clothes. Then, when we resent the picture-taking and stupid questions, you get angry."

"Got it all figured out, don't you?"

"Near enough. We like things the way they are."

"What about you?" he asked. "Aren't you trying to make changes, bring new ways to your people? Make their lives better?"

"It's not the same. I want to help—" Too late,

she realized the trap she'd fallen into. The man was too smart by half. Why hadn't she realized where the conversation was heading? And why did she care what Cassavettes thought about her, anyway?

"If we're going to work together," he said reasonably, "we need to get past assigning blame."

Once again, he was right.

Their relationship was based on mutual need. Once Jimmy returned, she'd have no need for an extra assistant. She wondered why the prospect suddenly depressed her.

"I'm sorry," she said. This time she meant it.

He stuck out his hand. "Truce?"

"Truce."

He wrapped his fingers around hers. "One question."

"All right."

"Who's Janet named for?"

Chapter Four

Nick's respect for Rachel grew with each day. If he thought she were going to hand over all the drudge work to him and keep the easier assignments for herself, he couldn't have been more wrong. If she drove him hard, it was no more than she did herself.

The truth was, there was a lot to admire about Rachel Small Deer. She was stubborn, feisty as all get-out, and too impulsive for her own good. But she was also warm and caring and generous. He made a face. He was making her out to sound like some girl scout, and that was the *last* thing he felt about her.

When she told him that Cal Jenkins had named his favorite sow after his dead wife, they enjoyed a good laugh together and he added a sense of humor to her list of virtues.

He was beginning to understand that her job was much more than simply a way to make a living. It demanded an energy, passion, and commitment that up until now he'd associated only with art. Once again, he was reminded how narrow his outlook had been, how self-absorbed his world.

She waded knee-deep in mud to draw blood from a cow. She worked eight hours straight trying to save a colt that had hopelessly tangled itself in a coil of barbwire. When she had to put it down, she'd done so with compassion, eyes dry and hands steady.

It was only later that he'd discovered her closeted in the back room of the clinic, crying as if her heart would break. That glimpse of vulnerability shook him as nothing else could. He started to reach out, to touch her arm, then thought better of it. She wouldn't welcome the gesture or the comfort he wanted to offer.

She was a puzzle—this woman who worked from dawn until dark for very little money and even less respect. The animal testing was the bread and butter of her operation, but the heart of her work belonged to the small ranchers and farmers. She practically gave away her services, accepting hams or chickens or a basket of vegetables in return for her work. The ranchers and farmers treated her with a wariness that bordered on distrust.

When he mentioned that to her, she shrugged.

"My father was the vet around here for years. They accepted him. I'm another matter."

"Because you're a woman?"

"Partly. They see me as the little girl who used to follow her father around, getting in the way. They can't accept that I might be able to help them."

"Why do you keep trying?"

"They're my friends. My family."

For Rachel, it was as simple as that.

She fulfilled her promise to him with scrupulous care. Somewhat to his surprise, Rachel was always charitable as she showed him around the reservation. Much as she tried to detest him on a personal level, she was unfailingly positive when she introduced him to family and friends.

She didn't want to. He understood that. But she'd given her word and she'd keep it or die trying. He understood that as well. And respected it.

Rachel continued to take him with her on her weekly visits to the reservation.

Most of the people were eager to meet him and wanted to pose for him. Chubby-cheeked babies, tribal chiefs, middle-aged housewives—each had their own appeal. But none sparked the interest in him that he needed to get his art back on track.

"Rachel! Rachel!" The piping voice had both of them turning their heads.

The small boy trotting toward them held something squirming in his arms. When he drew nearer,

Nick could make out a coyote pup. Every story he'd ever read about wild animals and rabies came flooding back, but Rachel didn't appear worried.

The boy handed the animal to Rachel. "He got his leg caught in a trap. You'll fix him, won't you?"

Nick noticed that Rachel held the pup firmly but kept it at a prudent distance. "I'll do my best." She wrapped the animal in a blanket she kept in the back of her truck and headed to the clinic.

Nick finally managed to voice his fears aloud. "Aren't you afraid of rabies?"

"It's always a threat, but this little fellow doesn't look like he's infected." One hand on the steering wheel, she made an angry gesture with the other. "Steel traps. If I had my way, they'd be abolished."

Once they reached the clinic, she had the animal on the examination table within seconds. Deep grooves worked their way between her brow. "The Native Americans believe that if you take an animal's breath, you will preserve his spirit."

Nick understood. She was going to have to put the animal down. Under the circumstances, it was the kindest thing she could do.

She worked quickly, running her hands over the pup's trembling body. "I can save him."

"Look at him. He can't run. He'll be a target for any predator out there."

"We can't let that happen. If I set the bone, put a cast on the leg, he may make it."

"You can't save everything."

"No. But I can save *this* animal."

"Stubborn woman."

"Are you going to help or are you going to stand around and criticize?"

She didn't give him time to answer but thrust a couple of instruments into his hands. She worked quickly, but carefully all the same. The coyote's life depended upon her skill.

His hand brushed hers as they worked together over the small creature. The awareness that zinged through him caused him a moment of alarm. As soon as it was safe to do so, he pulled his hand away.

Rachel appeared oblivious to what had happened. He ought to be grateful she hadn't noticed the sparks that sizzled in the air. An hour later, she washed up at the sink. "Thanks."

"You're incredible." He eyed the pup, now sleeping peacefully, a small cast encasing his hind leg.

"It feels good, doesn't it?" she asked. "Saving something you thought was lost."

Yeah. It feels good. Real good. He wondered if Rachel might help him save him as well.

The outing had reaped more information about Rachel Small Deer: Committed. Compassionate. Occasionally short-tempered.

He had a lot to think about during the next few

days. Rachel had given him a glimpse into life on the reservation, and he understood that he had seen only the tip of the iceberg. It was up to him to look beneath the surface and see the deeper meaning. But a certain vet kept intruding in his thoughts, churning them up, and then spitting them out.

He hadn't touched his paints in days. He'd stopped trying to fool himself. The hunger inside him to paint was as strong as ever, but he feared his talent had dried up.

He continued to accompany Rachel on her rounds. He'd discovered something. He needed her. Not just for introductions, but for the energy she brought to her work, her life. Maybe, just maybe, he could catch a bit of the joy she experienced in even the smallest things.

When the last day of the first week drew to a close, he found her holed up behind the desk. Worry lines etched themselves between her brows as she sorted through the papers littering the battered desk.

Bills, he thought, as he drew closer. A stack of them, by the look of it. She looked weary, her gold skin pale under the lamplight. Vulnerable. The word astounded him. He'd seen her as tough, invincible. Now she looked fragile. Fragile and weary. The vulnerability he saw in her eyes did strange and unwelcome things to him.

He didn't want to see it, the worry and fatigue she tried so hard to hide. It was foolish, he told himself, to get emotionally involved with his employer and guide.

"Rough day?" he asked, careful to keep his voice even.

She turned and pushed a hand through her hair. "Yeah."

He gestured to the pile of bills. "Those can wait. You're exhausted."

Her laugh was short. "Unfortunately, they can't." She flipped one over, and he read the PAST DUE notice on it.

"Look, maybe I could—"

"You're not going to offer me a loan, are you?"

Until a moment ago, he had been. "I guess not."

"Good." Her smile came quickly but failed to reach her eyes.

"Are things that bad?"

"I can manage," she said shortly.

He wondered about that. He knew she gave away supplies and a great deal of her work. Many of the area farmers couldn't afford to pay for her services, and others flat-out refused. Still others offered goods in barter. Any way you looked at it, she couldn't be making enough to earn a decent living.

"It'll all work out." She lifted a shoulder in a casual gesture.

He imagined she thought her shrug came off as unconcerned, but he wasn't deceived. If she'd let him, he'd pay her for the time she spent showing him around. When he'd been foolhardy enough to suggest that once, she'd nearly bitten his head off, reminding him of their deal.

Pride? The lady had it in spades.

Needing to touch her, he skimmed a knuckle down her cheek. Her eyes widened as she stared up at him.

Stupid, he thought. *That was stupid.* Hadn't he resolved to keep the relationship strictly business?

Rachel had turned her attention back to the bills, and he was grateful. He didn't want her reading anything more into the impulsive gesture.

Her normally cheery disposition was conspicuously absent before eight A.M. Rachel believed in honoring all nature's creations, but those early hours . . . She rubbed the sleep from her eyes and muttered something uncomplimentary about people who called before six A.M.

A restless night left her out of sorts. She told herself her sudden fit of nerves was no more than the result of a sleepless night. The lie rubbed uneasily against her conscience as she acknowledged that her night hadn't been actually sleepless but filled with dreams about a certain brown-eyed artist.

How had she allowed the man to infiltrate her dreams? It was bad enough that she spent far too many hours thinking of him. And that was another thing she was spending too many hours doing—staring into space.

She pulled back the curtains and let the morning sun stream into the small kitchen tucked into a corner of the loft. She wrapped her hands around a mug of coffee, warming them. Even though temperatures in the desert could top a hundred degrees during the day, early mornings were chilly.

Nick was occupying far too much of her thinking and attention, and she resolved to push him out of her mind. But that was easier said than done. Especially since they had a date for tonight. When he'd suggested dinner followed by a drive through the desert, she'd accepted.

The desert didn't appeal to everyone, she thought, staring out the window to the vastness beyond. The knowledge that Nick shared her preference warmed her. He'd managed to surprise her. Again.

No, the desert wasn't for everyone. Its beauty was a demanding one. No rolling hills or leaf-laden trees softened the harsh edges of the land. It bespoke strength, exacting a matching one by those who chose to make their homes there.

When she let herself into the clinic just before 7:00, the phone was already shrilling.

The call was about one of the staples of a country vet's life: a cow down with mastitis. Modern antibiotics had eliminated the worst of the infection, but some animals still managed to contract it, usually those housed in old, ill-equipped barns.

Attempts to convince some of the old-timers to keep their barns germ-free had met with little success. What had worked for their fathers and their fathers before them was good enough for them, they maintained with staunch belief.

She left a note for Sally and took off.

Ben Winslow had a good heart, but he was so firmly rooted in the past that Rachel doubted she'd ever find a way past his outdated practices. She treated the cow, whose udder was so distended that it dragged the floor of the barn, the reason it had become infected.

"Apply this salve morning and night, after you finish your milking." With little hope that he'd accept it, she shoved a small tube of ointment at him.

"Don't need it." He ignored her outstretched hand, broke a piece of straw in half, and sucked on one end. "Got my own medicine."

"Excuse me, Mr. Winslow," Rachel said with a patience that was starting to fray at the edges, "if you have your own medicine, why did you call me?"

"The wife said I ought to give you a chance. Did, and now I can do what I should have done in the first place." He tipped his hat. "Meaning no offense, ma'am."

"No offense taken," she said with more resig-

Desert Paintbox 67

nation than anger. "Look, why don't you try my medicine? If it works, that's fine and you pay me for it. If it doesn't, you're not out anything."

" 'Cept maybe a good cow."

She held onto her temper. "If your cow dies, you don't have to pay me."

"Weren't planning on paying much," he said around the straw in his mouth.

"I wasn't planning on charging much." She stuck out her hand, pointedly waiting until he took the ointment. "Do we have a deal?"

"Yeah." He shoved the small tube into his pocket.

She winced inwardly as he pumped her hand with his own beefy one.

The sun beat down with ruthless energy as she cleaned her instruments, burning away any trace of the earlier chill. She pushed her hat back and let the slight breeze cool her forehead.

Cold and heat all in one day. That was the desert. A land of contrasts and color and conflict. Those who made their homes there had to fight to survive. It was that struggle that forged their strength.

The brilliance of the eastern sky promised a scorcher, despite the gusts of wind that kicked up. She lowered her hat back in place. The desert held its own beauty, one that couldn't be dismissed or denied. Just as potent were its dangers. A man... or a woman... would be a fool to ignore them.

Her thoughts turned to Nick. He hadn't been able to accompany her today. Perversely, she missed his company.

Maybe it was that that prompted her to say yes when he'd asked her out to dinner. And maybe it was more basic than that—the attraction that had existed between them from the start, an attraction she hadn't wanted to acknowledge.

"It's not a date," Rachel said loudly an hour later in response to Sally's teasing.

"How is it not a date?"

"Because we agreed it wasn't a date."

Sally cocked her head to the side. "Let me make sure I have this right. You say it's not a date, and that makes it not a date. Right?"

"Right."

Sally smirked. "I've got news for you, honey. If it talks like a duck and walks like a duck, it's probably not a fish."

"Thanks." Rachel had no trouble understanding her friend. Sally was in love and eager to see the whole world in that same blissful state. She wasn't going to accept Rachel's meager explanation of her relationship with Nick. Well, that was too bad. Rachel didn't intend to fabricate a relationship that didn't exist just to satisfy her friend's fantasies.

"Haven't we wasted enough time? Seems like we have some reports to get out."

"Sure thing, boss," Sally said so meekly that Rachel had to laugh.

Together, they put in two hours filling out the seemingly never-ending reports that appeared to multiply overnight. After she signed her name to the last one, Rachel suggested, "Why don't you knock off for lunch? Things are slow enough without two of us sitting around on our hands."

Sally accepted eagerly. "Thanks."

"Seeing Charlie?" she teased as Sally all but ran out of the clinic.

Sally grinned. "You bet."

Rachel smiled after her assistant. She knew Sally was anxious to be with her boyfriend. For a moment, she wished she, too, had someone who could produce such a reaction within her, someone with whom to share lunch, an evening . . . a lifetime. Annoyingly, the image of Nick Cassavettes flickered through her mind. The memory of the sensations that shimmered up her arm when he took her hand wouldn't banish.

Annoyed with herself, she walked to the back room to check on her patient. The coyote pup looked up at her with wary eyes.

"Nobody's going to hurt you," she said, automatically adopting the soothing tones she used whenever she worked with an animal. Gently, she removed the small creature from its cage, checking the bandaged leg.

The leg appeared to be healing nicely. Another couple of weeks and she could return the animal to his home. She was softhearted enough to want to keep all the wounded creatures she treated with her, to make sure they were safe. But the scientist in her knew that animals belonged in their own habitat.

Alone, she was assailed by doubts over her acceptance of a date with Nick. So what was she doing agreeing to have dinner with him?

She had no answer to that, at least, no good answer. With an impatient shake of her head, she shrugged off her preoccupation with a certain artist and methodically began going through the mail that accumulated each day.

The words blurred before her eyes, and Rachel wearily put the latest issue of *Veterinary Science* aside. She had been reading the same page for the last several minutes and had no more idea of what it said than she had when she had started. She knew the cause of her inability to concentrate.

Nick.

How had he managed to invade her mind so completely when she'd known him less than a dozen days? She had seen men equally as attractive before, but never such a compelling one. And never had one made such an impact on her as had this one.

She had accepted that if she was going to get through the testing, she needed help. She groaned inwardly. This kind of trouble she didn't need.

She had the life she'd always dreamed of—working with animals, helping the people she loved. But lately, she was growing aware of something missing. It was only coincidence that thoughts of Nick filled her mind at that moment, she assured herself.

The shipment of medicine she'd ordered had come in. Once again, she marveled at the men and women who had practiced veterinary medicine in the early years of the century. Without modern diagnostics and treatments, they had operated almost purely on instinct and trial and error.

Not that modern methods were infallible. Vets still encountered problems they couldn't answer and made mistakes, but she knew she was fortunate to have so many miracles at hand. Like the antibiotics that had just arrived. With them, she could treat mastitis and other ailments much more effectively than her ancestors had.

When Grandfather Ray showed up, she smiled in welcome. Following the death of her parents in a flash flood, her grandfather had raised her. One of the tribal elders, he had taken her part when she wanted to go away to school, defending her against those who accused her of growing apart from their traditions.

"Keep your dream," he'd told her that day when she was ready to climb aboard the bus to take her away from everything and everyone she knew and loved. "Dreams give us light. And knowledge."

Rachel had stored away the words to be taken out and examined later. The words had stood her in good stead, keeping alive her goal to become a veterinarian when all the odds were stacked against her.

"I like your young man," he said after giving her the herbs he'd collected.

Her hand tightened around the pouch she held. "Young man?" she repeated in an admirably bewildered tone. "I don't know who you're talking about."

Grandfather Ray looked disappointed. "The young man you brought to the reservation. The one who could not look away from you."

She managed a chuckle. "He's not my young man. I explained to you. We're helping each other out."

"My eyes are old, not blind," her grandfather said. "He looks at you with the warmth of a thousand summers."

Her grandfather was a smart man, his years only adding to the wisdom. But he was wrong about this. Nick didn't feel anything but gratitude to her. Circumstances had thrown them together. Circumstances and mutual need.

Rachel was very much afraid that Nick was in her thoughts to stay. The only question was, did she want to let him in her life?

Desert Paintbox

She had a full measure of women's intuition. She could feel it humming inside her that very moment.

But she was used to good-looking men and knew it wasn't the physical package that made him so compelling. Perhaps it was the expression in his eyes.

The arrogance she might have expected from a man of his talent was conspicuously absent. The gaze he leveled at her was steady and clear, radiating integrity and strength. He was, she realized in a flash, a man you could count on.

It wasn't as if this was a real date, she reminded herself for the hundredth time. But her attempt to keep her imagination in check seemed doomed to failure.

Nick hadn't slept worth a darn, thanks to a certain dark-haired vet. He wanted to blame his wayward thoughts on a full moon, but last night's sky had been an unbroken strip of black velvet.

His scowl deepened. Since when had he started thinking in terms of full moons and black velvet nights? Since he'd given into the impulse to touch her cheek, that's when.

Rachel Small Deer was the last woman he wanted to get involved with. She was pushy, opinionated, and altogether too certain she had all the answers. She had a mouth on her that wouldn't quit and a way of pushing his buttons.

She also cared about others. He'd learned firsthand how she went out of her way to help anyone who needed it. Word of it had spread. Los Cincos didn't have any secrets.

And if he didn't start keeping his mind on business and off the pretty vet, he'd give the town a whole new subject to gossip about.

He had a date with her tonight. He was taking her to dinner, by way of a thank-you for showing him around the reservation and town.

He didn't delude himself into believing it could be anything more, that *they* could be anything more. She was an attractive woman, one who challenged him, intrigued him, demanded that he leave behind his old way of thinking and embrace a new one.

Forcibly, he reminded himself that he had no interest in Rachel other than an enjoyable dinner date.

Yeah, right, an inner voice mocked.

He'd been interested in Rachel from the moment he'd met her. She was a mass of contradictions, soft and tough, canny and still naive in many ways. And everything he learned about her only made him want to know more.

They were adults. Attracted to each other, but that was all. All that he would let it be. But he wasn't as sure of himself as he wanted to be.

Chapter Five

When Lucy came down with colic late that afternoon, Rachel canceled what appointments she could, rescheduled others, and left her cell phone number with Sally for emergencies.

Rachel had learned to ride on Lucy's back. She'd taken up jumping and trick riding and needed a more spirited horse, but she never forgot Lucy. When the mare became too old for day-long rides through the desert, Rachel still visited her, never failing to bring an apple.

Nick showed up at the barn, taking her by surprise. "Sally told me what happened."

She flushed. She'd completely forgotten about the dinner. "Our dinner . . . I'm sorry."

He waved a hand in dismissal. "What can I do?"

The offer of help nearly undid her. "She can't get up. . . . If a horse doesn't get up . . ." She didn't finish. Her voice wobbled, a shaky, quivery sound that she hated because of the weakness it betrayed.

He pulled her into his arms. The surprise of it raced through her. Then came other surprises, one on top of another. The feel of being held against a man's strong chest. The scent of that same man—soap and the earthy smells of a day spent working with animals.

He pressed his lips to her hair. "It's going to be all right," he murmured, the words barely audible. But she caught them and the concern behind them.

He emptied the sack. A thermos of coffee. Blankets. Even a pillow. Her eyes filled with tears at the thought and care he'd shown for her.

"Come on," he said. "We might as well get comfortable."

"You don't have to stay," she said. She dreaded the thought of the long hours alone spent standing vigil over Lucy. But she couldn't expect Nick to understand how much her old friend meant to her. Or to spend the night in a cold, drafty barn.

Nick took her hands and pressed them between his own. "I want to stay."

She looked at him, his features slightly blurred in the dim light of the barn. She'd misjudged him . . . in so many ways. How had she thought him arrogant or selfish?

He knew how much Lucy meant to her, how she'd blame herself if the mare didn't pull through.

She reached for his hand and laced her fingers through his.

Nick felt the gentle warmth in her touch. He was the one who was supposed to do the comforting tonight.

He studied her face, frowning at what he saw there. The gray cast to her skin, the blankness of her eyes worried him. How long had it been since she'd had anything to eat?

"I'll get you something to eat," he said.

She thanked him with a tired smile that didn't reach her eyes.

In the postage stamp of a kitchen in her loft, he pulled out a carton of eggs and scrambled them with some cheese and green pepper. It wouldn't win any awards with the Heart Association, but it was filling and hot. Returning in a few minutes with a kettle of tea and the plate of food, he found Rachel checking Lucy's vitals. "She's breathing easier now."

He heard the note of cautious optimism in her voice, the hope that wouldn't quit despite the odds against the mare's recovery. He nodded, noting the steady rise and fall of Lucy's sides. He dropped to the floor, propping his back against the wall. "Come here," he said, patting the spot beside him.

She hesitated only a moment before dropping to the ground. Together, they ate the dinner that neither wanted. Once they'd finished, he pulled her to him, settling her into the shelter of his arms.

He shifted so that her head rested comfortably against his shoulder. When he pulled a blanket over her, she frowned.

"I'm not going to sleep. I have to stay awake and watch Lucy."

"I know. But there's no sense freezing to death."

She nodded, her eyes drifting shut until she snapped them open. He smiled to himself. She fought her exhaustion as she fought anything that stood in her way. He could see the struggle on her face. Before much longer, she slipped into sleep. He felt her every shift and sigh as she nestled against him. Gently, he pulled off her boots and tucked the blanket around her.

She seemed younger, more vulnerable as sleep softened the stubborn set of her jaw. Incredibly long lashes rested upon her cheeks. To soothe them both, he gave in to the temptation to brush his lips against her forehead. She stirred but didn't waken.

With Rachel curled at his side, he was reminded how small she was . . . how delicate. He could easily encircle her wrist with his thumb and forefinger and still have room left over. Delicate wasn't a word he normally associated with her. She was so vibrant, so full of energy and life that he forgot just how little she really was.

Unable to help himself, he reached for her hand. Calluses pocked the pale gold skin. She worked too hard, he thought. The life of a country vet wasn't for the weak or faint-hearted. She didn't let her size keep her from doing her job, though. He'd seen her tackle jobs that would intimidate men twice her weight. She had more grit than anyone he'd ever met.

Realizing just where his thoughts were taking him, he frowned. He didn't need that kind of complication in his life. He was fighting to reclaim what was left of his talent. A woman like Rachel . . . any woman . . . was bound to interfere with that. He had to concentrate on what brought him to Los Cincos in the first place. Rachel and he had struck a deal; they'd help each other out and then go their separate ways. That was what he wanted, what he needed.

She started in her sleep, the reflexive jerk causing her fingers to tense around his. He soothed them with his thumb, until she relaxed. He kept her hand in his, finding the clasp oddly comforting.

Lucy turned her head, her chocolate brown eyes seeming to ask his intentions. ''It's okay, girl. I'll take care of her.''

Rachel awoke to the sound of gentle nickering. She turned her head. For the first time in eighteen hours, Lucy got to her feet. Rachel started toward her. Only then did she realize that she was curled in Nick's arms. Gently, she freed herself, careful not to wake him.

She got to her feet unsteadily, her legs numb from

the long hours on the cold floor, but the discomfort couldn't dim her elation over seeing Lucy standing.

"Lucy." Rachel wrapped her arms around the mare's neck and received a nuzzle in return.

Giving an impatient snort, Lucy stuck her head in her feed box.

"Hey, girl," Rachel murmured, rubbing the mare's neck. "You gave us a real scare. But you're gonna be all right. Not too much at once," she said when the mare kept right on eating.

The sound of her huge teeth chomping on her feed was music to Rachel's ears. She nudged the animal aside and laughed when Lucy tried to nip her.

After assuring herself that Lucy wasn't going to overeat, Rachel stretched and wiped her eyes. Her nose wrinkled as she caught a whiff of herself. After twenty-four hours in the same clothes, she smelled like one of the animals she treated.

Lucy had kept down her food and was fretting to go for a run.

"Not yet," Rachel said, her hands gentle as she groomed the mare. The repetitious motion smoothed away the rough edges left by a night spent in a barn stall, soothing her as well as her old friend.

Lucy responded with a soft whinny.

Rachel gave her a final pat and led her outside. With a pat to her rump, she let Lucy go. Lucy took off at a trot for the far corner of the corral. The sight of her running filled Rachel with a sense of wonder. Only the day before Lucy had been down, giving every appearance of never being able to get up again.

A faint breeze cooled her skin. Dawn speared pink fingers of light through the cloud-laden sky. She looked up, hoping the clouds meant rain. Like most country folk, she followed the weather. The county had been too long without moisture, and draught conditions were ripe. But little could ruin her mood this morning.

Though she'd been born here, Rachel never tired of the sunrises, the colors so brilliant as to rival that of the most spectacular scenery in the world. Dotted with cacti and inhabited by scorpions and gila monsters, the land was as harsh and unforgiving as the climate, but it held its own beauty. And she wouldn't trade it for all the lush greenery in the world.

She swiped her hands down her jeans, managing to dislodge some of the dirt but none of the smell.

"That's not going to help much."

She spun around to find Nick watching her and realized how she must look. And smell. She put a hand to her hair and tried to smooth it into some kind of order.

"Don't. You look beautiful."

She stared at him. A day's growth of beard shadowed his jaw. His eyes were blurry with fatigue. And she wanted very much for him to kiss her.

As though he had read her thoughts, he was at her side in two long strides. "There's something I've been wanting to do all night," he said.

When he moved his hand to cup her neck, she knew what was coming. The intent in his eyes was obvious as was the shortness of his breath. Gently, so very gently, he fitted his lips to hers. He deepened the kiss, shaping his mouth against hers. It was a meeting of lips but so much more, a giving and taking.

She concentrated on breathing. Breathing in and breathing out.

She gave herself up to the kiss.

He was the one to break the sweet contact, to raise his head and smile.

When he raised his head he was shaken. The kiss wasn't supposed to have been anything but a quick caress. It had taken him by surprise. He hadn't expected it. Least of all did he expect his reaction to it. "I'm sorry." He felt as awkward as a schoolboy caught kissing his best girl on the playground.

"Don't apologize. I enjoyed it."

Her honesty startled him almost as much as did the kiss. She was as guileless as a child, with her huge eyes gazing straight into his heart. He urged her to him, his hands resting at her waist.

He forgot that he was here in New Mexico for a few months only. He forgot that Rachel Small Deer was off limits, that he had no place for a woman in his life. He forgot everything . . . everything but the woman in his arms.

He didn't try to kiss her again. He was content to hold her, to feel her heart beat a rapid tattoo against his chest. Words were unnecessary, which was good, because he couldn't think of a thing to say.

When Sally showed up with a message that Rachel had a telephone call, he dropped his hands from her shoulders and Rachel stepped self-consciously away.

He drew in a deep breath, not sure whether he was sorry or relieved by the interruption. A little of both, he decided. What did he think he was doing, anyway? He had no business becoming involved with a woman like Rachel.

He was drawn to her in a way that defied logic. It was a rough time. His reaction to her couldn't be trusted. The wisest course of action would be to forget those few moments of intimacy had ever happened.

Which was just what he intended to do.

* * *

Rachel looked up as Nick let himself into the clinic. She felt her smile bloom from the inside out at his presence.

He must have gone back to his studio, for he was freshly shaved. Gone were the whiskers. Creased chinos and a denim shirt replaced the crumpled clothes from last night.

"Last night . . . thank you. For everything." Did that stammering bit of nonsense come from her? She was remembering how it felt to have his arms around her, his lips a scant inch from her own.

"You're welcome."

For a moment, she imagined she knew what he was thinking. He didn't smile, didn't make a move toward her, but something in the depth of his gaze told her that he, too, was remembering what it felt like to hold her, to kiss her.

The steady drizzle of rain, worth its weight in gold, had canceled all but the most urgent of her appointments.

She checked the coffeepot and found the last of yesterday's brew. She heated it up, took a gulp, and shuddered. It was as awful as she remembered. She handed a cup to him and warned, "Drink at your own risk."

He eyed it warily. "Yesterday's?" When she nodded, he put the cup down on the desk. "I don't think my stomach can handle another cup of that. What's in it, anyway?"

"We put a little fertilizer in it for fiber."

Nick laughed. Then he sobered and held out his arms.

She walked into them and let her head rest against his shoulder. He smelled of soap and the scent that was uniquely his. He drew her closer until she could scarcely breathe. When she drew a long, shuddering breath, he released her.

"This could become a habit," he said.

His words had her cheeks heating with color.

He traced a gentle finger along her jaw. A faint tremor fluttered in her stomach.

She felt like they'd reached a new understanding. Holding out her hand, she expected him to take it in his. Instead, he brought it to his lips and pressed a gentle kiss in the center of her palm.

"We . . . I, uh . . ." Her voice was as befuddled as her mind.

Nick saved her further embarrassment. "I have to go to Denver and see my agent. Can Fred stay with you for the day?"

Only then did she notice the big dog who sprawled by the door.

"He gets nervous when there's a storm," Nick explained.

Fred gave a mournful grunt as thunder rumbled in the distance. Desert storms rarely lasted long, but they could be violent.

She and Sally worked together for the rest of the

day. She was grateful for the routine of it. The ordinary chores helped restore her poise that had taken a beating under the assault of Nick's kiss.

The wet weather worked against her. To her chagrin, the phone had remained stubbornly silent. No emergency calls to occupy her attention. And her calendar was depressingly empty. In short, she was stuck with her own thoughts. And all those thoughts centered around a brown-eyed artist and the way he made her feel.

She had to keep him at a distance, if she were to concentrate on her job. No more casual touches. No more bone-melting kisses.

She looked up to find Sally regarding her speculatively. Her friend was smiling broadly. "You look like you're a million miles away," Sally said. "Or maybe just from here to Denver. Thinking about a certain artist?"

Rachel bent her head in an effort to conceal the telltale color that she felt heat her cheeks.

"Being in love is great," Sally said. "You oughta try it."

"I'll leave that to you. Besides, one of us has to keep their feet on the ground around here. The way you look right now, I guess it had better be me." It was true. Sally was glowing.

"My head may be in the clouds, but my feet are firmly planted right here," she said, and then promptly disproved her words by tripping over Fred, who had parked himself by the desk.

Rachel kept a straight face.

Sally gave Fred a disgusted look. "That mutt manages to be wherever I am. How'd we get stuck baby-sitting him, anyway?"

"Nick had to fly to Denver to meet with his agent. He didn't want to leave Fred alone." Rachel lowered her voice. "Fred gets nervous during storms."

As if to prove her words, Fred whined at the roar of thunder. The sizzle-boom of lightning quickly followed by another roll of thunder sent Fred scurrying under the desk. Fur bristling, he started to whimper.

Rachel crouched to pet him. "It's all right, you big baby."

"Leave him," Sally advised. "He's underfoot enough as it is. Maybe I can get some work done if he stays there."

Rachel wasn't fooled. Sally had the softest heart around. When Rachel saw her friend sneaking a bite of her sandwich to Fred, she kept her smile carefully under wraps.

When Nick returned to collect Fred later that evening, Rachel sought to keep him there for a few minutes longer. "How was your trip?"

"Long." He didn't elaborate, and she took the

hint to keep her questions to herself. "How was Fred?"

She gestured to the desk. "He spent most of the day hiding under there."

Nick's smile flashed, warming the distant expression in his eyes. "Thanks for keeping him."

"No problem." She hesitated. "Would you like to come for dinner some night? I owe you that after last night."

"I'd like that."

Things changed after that. More precisely, *she* had changed, Rachel acknowledged. She had opened herself to Nick and to her own feelings.

Years ago, still in vet school, she'd been engaged to another student of mixed heritage like herself. She had passed the national board exam and he hadn't. He'd blamed her. Their relationship had deteriorated after that. Looking back, she understood their attraction lay in their common heritage rather than genuine feeling. It had been with relief that she'd ended the engagement.

Since then, she'd kept her heart whole and focused her energies on the dream she'd harbored since childhood. Now she wondered if there were room in her life for another dream as well.

Chapter Six

The decision to waste a few minutes having a cup of tea at a local café was an impulsive one. As soon as Rachel sat down, though, she knew it had also been a wise one.

She needed time to think about Nick and what was happening between them. She couldn't do that when she was with him. His very presence turned her brain to mush.

That Nick wasn't an ordinary man, she'd already admitted. That he had the power to slip past the barriers she'd so carefully erected, she still had to acknowledge.

The man was clearly a magician, turning her feelings inside out and her life upside down. Hadn't she decided that she would concentrate on her career? After all those years spent going to school, she owed it to herself to build up her practice.

Now, though, her thoughts focused on a very special man.

Until he'd found his way into her life, she'd been content. Not happy, perhaps, but content. And that was the way she wanted it.

Wasn't it?

The question taunted her with unrelenting persistence, demanding she give it attention. The question, and it was a big one, was if she let him into her life, what then? What became of her carefully ordered existence? Did she dare take that chance? Did she dare *not* to?

Was it a good feeling, being the other half of a couple? Or did you have to give up part of yourself to unite with another? Was it worth the risk? Once, she'd thought she knew. Now, she wasn't sure.

Would it be the same if he kissed her again? Would she feel that same quiet intensity when he touched his lips to hers? Softly demanding. Sweetly inviting. *Would* he kiss her again? More important, did she want him to?

The question gave way to others.

What would it be like to know you could stretch out your hand and someone else would take it in his own? She looked at her hand, remembering the way it had fit inside Nick's. His hand had been hard. Like the man himself. But there would be gentleness, too. It was that dichotomy that intrigued her. Strength tempered by gentleness.

He wasn't an easy man to know. Instinctively, she knew he wouldn't make a relationship easy either. He would be demanding, at times asking more than she could give, and at others giving more than she ever dreamed. Risky, that's what he was. And a woman foolish enough to get involved with him would risk her heart.

No, she didn't need a man in her life right now. But sometimes . . . sometimes . . . she wished there were someone special. Someone to share the good times with as well as the bad. Someone to chase away the loneliness. Someone to . . . love.

For a fraction of a heartbeat, she reflected on what it would be like to be cherished, really cherished. Would his kisses always stir her as his last one had? Or would she grow tired of them, tired of him, as the initial thrill faded and familiarity set in?

No!

That the answer came without hesitation disturbed her. Even more disturbing was the fact she was thinking about him at all. Thoughts of him invaded her working hours as well as her dreams.

She took another sip of tea, soothed by the mild herbal flavor.

Confused by the conflicting emotions warring within her, she shook her head in an attempt to wipe away the clash between feeling and reason. She didn't need Nick Cassavettes or his particular brand of charm. That's all it was, she assured herself. A way with words and a good-looking face. Well, they wouldn't work with her.

By the time she finished her tea, she had successfully managed to set her priorities straight. Her work demanded her full attention. She assured herself that was what she wanted. She didn't have time for a relationship—or anything else—with Nick. That settled, she felt better.

She folded up her thoughts and headed back to the office.

Sally looked up from the computer screen and flashed Rachel a smile. Her smile faded as she studied Rachel's face.

"It's the artist, isn't it?" Sally asked after they exchanged small talk.

Rachel felt Sally's probing gaze and almost wished her friend weren't so perceptive.

"You're in love with him."

Sally's words hit Rachel like a douse of cold water. In love with Nick? They'd known each other for only a few weeks. She admitted that she found him attractive, that she had even come to care for him. But love . . . That was something else.

Rachel envied her friend her uncomplicated life. Sally had had the same boyfriend since seventh grade. She knew what she wanted from life and went after it with no detours. She wasn't plagued with doubts or questions.

A trace of annoyance clouded her eyes. She

wasn't looking for a relationship, and even if she were, a man like Nick wouldn't stay in Los Cincos for long.

She found herself voicing her doubts to Sally.

"He might surprise you," Sally said.

Rachel forced her attention back to the monthly report. The business was operating in the black—by a narrow margin, to be sure, but a profit all the same. If she could only keep it that way for the next few months, she'd be in good shape for the slow winter months.

She worked her way through the quarterly tax forms, but her mind was far away. She kept at it for another hour, paying bills and balancing the books. At last, she shoved her chair back and stood. The hours of sitting at the desk had caused her legs to cramp. She grimaced as she pushed herself to her feet, her legs stinging with a thousand pinpricks.

Many people had yet to accept her. And her salary was too frequently a couple of fryer hens or hams. She reminded herself that acceptance by the hardy folk who made their home in the desert took time. And she hadn't gone into veterinary medicine to make a fortune. As long as she could buy supplies for her practice and keep her tin can of a truck running, she wouldn't complain.

When the phone shrilled, she reached for it.

"Yes," she agreed after listening to Ben Winslow harangue her for twenty minutes. She rolled her eyes at Sally. "I can see your point." She'd charged him only the cost of her medicine, donating her time and skill.

She put down the phone with a sigh. Spending money on animals still went against the grain with many of the old-timers.

Sally gave her a sympathetic smile. "Ben Winslow?"

Rachel grimaced. "Yeah. Said he used that ointment I gave him for his cow but figured a bit of lard worked just as good." Her sigh came out as a strangled laugh. "I guess this is why we get those fat paychecks."

"Fat?" Sally laughed. "Yours is anorexic." Her young face grew troubled. "How are you supposed to make a living when you don't charge for your work?"

Rachel had often wondered the same thing. "It's not so bad," she said at last. "I get to do a job I love. And I do all right."

"Sure you do. That's why you're overdrawn at the bank." Her assistant's face reddened. "I didn't mean to pry," she added quickly. "I was opening the clinic mail and got your bank statement by mistake."

Rachel shrugged. She didn't have any secrets from Sally. "I'll make it right."

"You wouldn't have to if people paid you what they owe."

"Would you have me turn away someone who had a sick animal?"

The quick shake of Sally's head had her smiling. "See? You're as soft a touch as I am. Besides, I like what I'm doing right now."

"And Nick? Do you like him too?"

Rachel pretended an interest in the gouges that scarred her desk as she tried to ignore the quivery sensations that danced down her spine. "Nick's nice enough."

Sally snorted. "Don't hand me that. There's been something between you two right from the start. I'd say that you and he are more than friends."

"Are you asking if I love him?" Rachel heard herself ask the words as if from a distance.

"Do you?"

She took refuge in briskness. "You've got love on the mind. Nick and I enjoy each other's company. That's all there is to it."

Sally refrained from saying anything more, and Rachel was grateful for her friend's tact. It was hard enough adjusting to the idea that she might be falling in love with Nick Cassavettes. It took all of her self-discipline to concentrate on her work for the rest of the day.

Her confidence restored, she could view the situation between herself and Nick more rationally. They were attracted to each other. It was a matter of chemistry, two people drawn to each other through no fault of their own. This dispassionate view of their relationship was heartening. Physical attraction was a commonplace thing. She had experienced it before. She would undoubtedly experience it again. For now, she would enjoy his company.

But Sally's question came back to taunt her in the long hours of the evening. Was she in love with Nick? All her fine resolve of earlier fled, and she was afraid she already knew the answer. Her insides tightened at the knowledge.

Emergencies, large and small, had crowded the day, and it was with a feeling of relief that she climbed the stairs to her loft. Nick was coming at 6:00, giving her time to have a bath and change clothes.

He'd accepted her invitation to dinner with flattering enthusiasm.

Nick was fast becoming the most important thing in her life. The admission came more easily than she anticipated, even after that little pep talk she'd given herself earlier. That, more than anything, worried her.

After a quick shower and clean clothes, she looked at her reflection in the mirror. She didn't *look* any different, she noted with relief. Surely a woman in love would look somehow different than she had before. Sally had been way off base with her crazy ideas.

Desert Paintbox 97

Nick gave a wolf whistle when she opened the door for him at 5:55. "How do you manage to look so good after working with animals all day?" he asked, drawing her close and brushing a kiss against her hair.

A tiny pulse throbbed at the base of her throat.

He smothered his face in her hair and breathed in its freshly washed scent. "You smell like honeysuckle," he said softly.

His breath tickled her neck. When his hands, which were resting on her shoulders, moved lower to caress her bare arms, she shivered.

"I'm glad you came tonight," she said. "I like being with you."

Her honesty, as open as the desert sky at night, touched him as nothing else could. No games for her.

She reached up to kiss him.

Tenderness, sweet as the lips he'd just kissed, curled inside him.

"Dinner'll be ready in a few minutes," she said, and headed to the small corner kitchen.

Interested, he looked around. The living area of the loft was as contradictory as its decorator. Native American rugs covered the floor. Impressionistic prints on the far wall drew the eye. Pillows the color of the desert sky at sunset plumped on a sofa promised comfort.

Two prints hung above the sofa. One was of the

desert at sunrise—a peaceful vista with the sun only a hint of rose. The other was the same scene at sunset, the sky streaked with vivid, bold shades, the land reflecting that same clash of color.

The effect was at once energetic and restful. He wondered if she knew how much of herself each painting revealed.

Again, he wondered at the woman who both exasperated him and intrigued him.

She spooned up bowls of stew and placed a basket of bread on the table.

They talked, about everything except his art. He was loathe to tell anyone that each attempt to paint since he'd moved to Los Cincos had met with failure. His agent had been brutally frank during Nick's last trip to Denver.

"You're losing it, pal," Jerry had said. "Get over what it is that's eating you and start painting." His shrug said that he couldn't help anymore.

Nick pushed the conversation from his mind.

"That was wonderful," he said after they'd finished the simple meal of Navajo bread and vegetable stew. Though he was a competent enough cook, he rarely bothered with anything for himself that didn't come from a can or the freezer.

When she had plied him with seconds of everything, she announced, "Time for dessert."

The fruit cobbler topped by ice cream melted in

his mouth. Unashamedly, he held out his bowl for more.

He insisted upon cleaning up. He made short work of the clearing away and joined her within a few minutes. It had been a long time since he'd had a friend. And that was what Rachel had become. A friend.

The phone rang, shattering the mood with its jarring sound. Rachel went to answer it.

Sally's voice came over the line. "Rachel. I'm sorry to break in on your evening, but the sheriff called. There's trouble over at Snow's place. The sheriff asks that you get over there pronto."

"I'm on my way."

Nick had joined her in the kitchen. Quickly, she explained the situation. "I'd better go. I told Sally I'd be right there."

"Uh-uh. *We'll* be right there."

"You don't have to. It's not part of our agreement."

His eyes darkened. "I'm not talking about any agreement," he said, his voice turning surprisingly rough without any warning. "Do you want company or not?"

"It's not your business."

"But you are."

Warmth suffused her at his words, but all she said was, "Give me five minutes to change." She made a hasty exit to the bedroom. Quickly, she slipped off the dress and pulled on jeans and a shirt.

He looked impressed when she reappeared within five minutes. "I didn't know there was a woman alive who could change clothes in five minutes."

She thought of the evening they'd shared, of what might have been if work hadn't interfered. Maybe they'd have taken a walk together. She'd always liked the desert at night and longed to share it with Nick. However, now wasn't the time for romantic strolls in the moonlight.

"I'll drive you," he said, reminding her of his earlier words.

"I don't know what I'm going to find or how long I'll be there." There was no need for both of them to spend the rest of the night in what was bound to be a nightmare.

"I'm not letting you go alone."

She didn't have time to argue over his choice of words and nodded shortly. She couldn't help the small jolt of pleasure Nick's presence gave her. Nor could she ignore the zing of awareness that shot through her when he took her arm as he helped her into the truck.

Nick stole a glance at her in the dim light of the truck. She was sitting very still, back ramrod straight, features rigidly composed. With each passing mile, though, he could sense her dread increasing, the tension mounting inside her.

He pulled the truck into the pitted driveway, helped her out, and started to the barn.

She gave him a curt order to stay put.

Nick watched her disappear into the house and had to remind himself that this wasn't his job. His hands clenched at his sides as he forced himself to wait. Rachel had made it clear she didn't need his help, and he wasn't going to interfere.

Seconds stretched into minutes. Desert sounds cut through the otherwise silent night. He strained to hear and cursed the promise he'd made to Rachel to wait.

The porch light had been left on, casting garish shadows over the yard. He looked about. Peeling paint, a rickety fence, and a broken-down pickup truck parked in the yard told of dreams gone sour.

He strained to hear but could pick up only the faint murmur of voices over the bawl of the wind. *Enough,* Nick decided. He sensed Rachel needed him. Promise or not, he couldn't stand by and do nothing. He strode past the house and, following the sound of raised voices, made his way to the far corner of the barnyard. He took in the scene at a glance and braced himself for the probable outcome.

Two mares, stripped down to bone, had been left to die. He shivered as the cold desert wind whipped across the field and stuffed his hands inside his pockets, all the while his respect for Rachel growing as he realized what she meant to do. The lady had grit, more than anyone he'd ever met.

Rachel looked at the poor beasts, too far gone to even protest when she examined them. There was nothing to be done for them, nothing that she could do. And because she felt like weeping, she kept her eyes dry. There'd be time enough for tears later. Right now, she had something more important to do.

Her movements deliberately calm, she pulled a hypodermic from her bag. It was a tool she always hoped she wouldn't have to use, one she used only after she'd done everything else she could do. And then she used it only after she silently prayed. She did both in a matter of minutes. Her hands didn't shake, she noted.

"You had no right to put down my mares," Snow blustered.

Nick started toward her when she put a hand up to stop him. She needed to face Snow alone.

She grabbed him by the shirt and pushed him against the fence, anger lending her strength. "You let those horses die. But you wouldn't even let them die with dignity, you had to let them suffer. You don't deserve to have animals in your care. And if I have anything to say about it, you won't."

The sheriff stepped in then. Wally Timmons had a commonsense approach to law enforcement that she appreciated. She'd rarely seen him angry or even ruffled. Now, though, his eyes were cold. His mouth thinned until it was nothing more than a white line, made paler still by the contrast of his dark skin.

"You're under arrest," he told Snow.

"What for?"

"Pure meanness," one of the ranch hands muttered under his breath.

Snow turned on him, beefy fists raised.

"That'll be enough of that," the sheriff said. He snapped handcuffs on Snow. "Animal endangerment. Animal cruelty. And I could tack on a few more if you keep on provoking me."

Rachel gathered up her supplies, her movements brisk, no-nonsense. They were her defense against the despair that threatened to engulf her. Putting down an animal was part of her job. Her head told her that she had no choice. But her heart . . . oh, her heart was another matter. Her head and her heart were at constant war as she struggled with maintaining the delicate balance between caring . . . and caring too much.

It was then that reaction set in. The trembling started in her knees and spread to her legs. She groped for something to hold on to.

Nick folded her in the shelter of his arms. How long they stayed that way, she couldn't have said.

"It's time to go," he said gently. He fitted his hand at her waist, and it was as if the warmth of his touch gave her the strength she needed.

She raised her gaze to see him better. His eyes mirrored the pain she knew must be reflected in her own. His hand was comforting against her back and the physical awareness nearly overwhelmed her. She quivered with a longing that distressed her. How could she respond like this in the midst of her misery? Reaction, she supposed.

"You ain't heard the last of this," Snow said.

Nick nearly stepped between the belligerent man and Rachel, then thought better of it.

She lifted her chin, her eyes shooting sparks. "No, Mr. Snow. *You* haven't heard the last of this."

The lady was a fighter, Nick thought. She'd make it through this. *They'd* make it through this. Together.

"Come on," Nick said. "Let's get you home."

She put one foot in front of the other. If she concentrated on the act of walking, maybe she could block out the pain.

Nick slanted a look at her, his eyes narrowed in concern as he took in the tight set of her mouth, the too-precise way she held herself. A yawn slipped from her lips before she could stifle it. Her skin was gray beneath its normal gold, her eyes weary. Her shoulders drooped, her legs trembling as she walked to her truck. He tightened his arm around her waist, wanting to give comfort, discovering he needed it as well.

She didn't sag against him, didn't seem to have the substance in her to give weight, but he kept his arm in place. She looked fragile enough to blow away then and there. Given the stiff wind that had kicked up, it didn't take much imagination to envision her torn from his arms and swept away.

He knew she was tired. It was there in her eyes, in the lines furrowed across her forehead. She'd never admit to it, though. He knew it, accepted it, and didn't try to change her. She was a fighter, he thought once again. Beneath her gentle manner and soft words, she was pure steel. Perhaps it was that which he admired most. She managed to be both wholly feminine and tough as nails at the same time.

Did she have any idea of how valiant she was? He doubted it. Rachel didn't waste time patting herself on the back. She was too busy doing what had to be done.

She didn't protest when he took the keys from her and drove back to the clinic. There, she went to the back room and began sterilizing her instruments. Her hands shook, he saw, as she reached for the hypodermic.

She looked tired enough to drop. And, if he wasn't mistaken, she knew it. But she kept doggedly at her grim task.

He wanted to snatch the hypodermic from her,

order her to go home and go to bed, but he kept silent. Everyone had his or her own way of defusing the tension after a bad situation. Some took refuge in drink; others slammed their fists into walls. And some, like Rachel, focused on work.

He ran a finger down her cheek. It was the sort of gesture, he realized, that could easily become a habit, a habit he couldn't afford. Those brief glimpses of vulnerability that she worked so hard to hide sent his protective feelings into overdrive. He wasn't sure he liked the feeling. Rachel was a friend. That was all.

When she finished, he all but pushed her out the door. "There's nothing more you can do here."

His words scraped a nerve, raw and exposed. There had been nothing she could do for the mares. Nothing at all. The knowledge tore at her heart.

She looked up to catch Nick watching her. The understanding in his eyes warmed her. He knew what she was feeling, she realized in a flash of gratitude. The frustration, the sense of helplessness, the anger.

"You're incredible," he said, the husky timbre of his voice doing funny things to her insides.

That had the effect of heightening the color in her cheeks. He tucked a strand of hair behind her ear, his fingers lingering there for a moment.

"Thanks. For being there." Her voice trembled, and a stray tear tracked down her cheek.

He didn't stop to think, to analyze. He simply folded his arms around her. The tears melted down her cheeks, dampening his shirt. Stunned, he recognized how good she felt in his arms. *How right.*

He pressed her closer, feeling her hair against his cheek, smelling the fragrance that was at once meadow-fresh and innocently alluring. He sensed her hesitation, the battle of emotions that kept her still, until she locked her arms around his waist and held on tight.

What had started as a simple gesture of comfort had quickly evolved into something different, something he was unwilling to define. He'd had the same feeling at Snow's ranch, but he couldn't understand how touching Rachel had evoked such a strong reaction, a reaction he felt was totally inappropriate, given the circumstances.

She was vulnerable. His jaw set, he reminded himself he had no business feeling this way, not about this woman. Not about any woman. So he held her, just held her. And prayed it would be enough. For both of them.

Chapter Seven

Even in her exhausted state, her mind registered the warmth in his eyes, the solid presence of him.

He tightened his arms around her. It had started as a simple embrace between friends, but another sort of awareness entered into it. He was holding her the way a man holds a woman. And she was returning the embrace, her arms wrapped around his lean middle, her head pressed against his shoulder.

She melted into him and forgot the ugliness they had just witnessed, forgot all the obstacles that stood between them, forgot everything but the feel of his arms holding her.

He was, she realized, a man she could count on. A man who would be there through whatever came. The feeling was a foreign one, yet she accepted it as right. That was the word she was searching for. *Right.*

Desert Paintbox

It had been years since she'd allowed himself to be that vulnerable, to accept sympathy from another human being. Granted, she had been hurting. It had been an instinctive reaction, one she didn't question or try to comprehend. For once, her heart, not her head, had been in control.

The realization was a sobering one.

He ended the embrace, but not before he skimmed his thumb along her knuckles. It was the simplest of gestures, a bare touch, yet her heart stuttered a bit before resuming its normal steady beat.

"I'm okay," she said.

She is a lot more than that, an inner voice whispered to him.

Her beautiful eyes, shiny with just-shed tears, gazed at him gratefully. She was hurting, and he ached to wipe the pain away. But equally strong was the desire to kiss away the last traces of tears, to kiss her slightly parted lips, to kiss *her*.

Inside the loft, Nick nudged her toward the sofa, gently pushed her down, and then headed to the kitchen.

"Let's go see what you have in the refrigerator. Food," he added at her blank look. "You need some."

She watched as he rummaged through her refrigerator and pulled out cheese and an avocado and then sliced them. He spread mayonnaise on leftover pieces of the Navajo bread and put the whole thing together.

"I make a pretty mean sandwich." He fixed a teasing look at her.

She pushed herself up. "You don't have to do this."

"No."

"Then why are you?"

"Because you needed someone. I was here." He shrugged as though to say it was that simple.

"It's not simple," she said in response to the unspoken words. It never was.

She was falling for him, she realized with a flash of panic, and sought to lighten the atmosphere. "You may not be as hopeless as I thought."

A wry smile skimmed his lips. "Thanks. I think."

She discovered she had an appetite after all and ate the sandwich he'd prepared.

"This is good."

"You expected burnt offerings maybe?"

An embarrassed smile skidded over her lips. "Something like that."

"A bachelor either learns to cook for himself or eat out a lot. After a few months of being on my own, I decided I'd better learn to cook in self-defense."

"I'm impressed."

"Do you feel like talking about it now?" he asked.

She took her time finishing the sandwich. "I don't know if I can." She gathered up the dishes and carried them to the sink.

He followed her. "Leave them."

"But—"

"Relax. They'll still be there in the morning." He settled back into the deep cushioned chair, squaring one leg over the other.

After a moment's hesitation, she did the same.

The memory of putting down the mares returned, and fresh tears spiked her lashes. Rachel pressed her fingers to her temples, willing the headache that had taken up residence to leave. Stubbornly, it persisted, taunting her with its tenacity.

Nick came to stand behind her. Strong fingers gently moved hers aside and began massaging the tender area. Slowly, the pain receded under his touch.

She sucked in her breath, unbearably moved by his lightest touch. She didn't dare let it show. She couldn't reach out for something as ephemeral as a man's comfort. His presence here was only temporary, a month, maybe two. He was with her now because she had needed someone and no one else was available. Why couldn't she remember that?

"Why did you insist on coming with me tonight?'' she asked when he moved to hunker down beside her.

His eyes were shadowed with distant memories. "Once I let someone I cared about go off on his own when I knew better. I should have been with him, but I had something I thought was more important to do."

"What happened?"

He was silent for so long that she thought he wasn't going to give an answer.

Ghosts, she thought, recalling her earlier impression. Nick carried his private ghosts with him. She wondered what she had to do with them.

"It was a long time ago." His tone, more than the words themselves, told her to back off.

She took the hint but couldn't stop the hurt that flickered in her eyes.

"Aw, heck." He picked her up and then sat down in her chair, settling her on his lap.

She turned slightly, wanting to see him. His face filled her vision, and she saw the little things she'd tried not to notice. The shape of his mouth, firm yet gentle; the quiet strength in the set of his jaw; the way a thin ring of black outlined his irises, making his eyes appear darker than ever.

"Nick..." She hesitated, unsure of what she wanted to say, even more unsure of what she *needed* to say. A tremor of longing shuddered through her, and she yearned to close the distance between them.

"Let it out," he said. His low voice stirred something within her. Resolutely, she tried to ignore it and found, to her consternation, that she couldn't.

She wasn't sure anything would ever be right again.

He eased back, tucking a finger beneath her chin to lift her face to his. He kissed one wet cheek, then the other.

She trembled under his touch, whether from emotion or strain, she wasn't sure. Fact was, she wasn't sure about anything. Not anymore. Not since Nick Cassavettes had found his way into her life.

Aware she still remained in his arms, Rachel flushed. She should resist. She should tell him to leave. She should . . .

She did none of those things. Whatever his faults, Nick had the knack of making her feel safe, protected. She accepted it because it was there. She'd learned a long time ago to change what she could and to accept what she couldn't.

How had he known that she needed to be held, simply held? He uttered no empty words that everything would be all right. For that alone, she was grateful. She wanted to thank him, to tell him . . . she looked into his eyes and knew he understood.

For this one time, she allowed herself the luxury of leaning on someone else. She was so tired. Tired of being strong, tired of being in control, tired of burying her feelings.

But it was more than that. Something about this man made her want things, things she hadn't even been aware of—until now. Nick Cassavettes was everything she wanted. And so much more.

She felt exposed, allowing him to see her like this. But when he held her with such gentleness, such compassion, she wanted only to stay in the warm haven of his arms.

She was totally vulnerable, stripped of her defenses by one Nick Cassavettes. She traced the shape of his face, trailing a finger along its sculpted strength as though to memorize its contours. As long as she lived, she would remember this moment. This man.

Warmth stole across her cheeks as she thought of Nick and the tenderness he'd shown her. He'd known what she needed and had quietly seen to it. His matter-of-factness had robbed it of anything more personal. Yet, she'd *felt* his concern.

Never before had Rachel allowed anyone to get as close to her, outside her family, as Nick had. Even with her fiancé, she'd never shared the intimacy of feelings that she had with Nick. The connection between them had happened so easily, so naturally that she hadn't even noticed it.

He felt sorry for her, she reminded herself. She would do well to keep things in perspective instead of longing for the impossible. Still, he'd kissed her the way a man kisses a woman.

Desert Paintbox 115

Nick, she realized in a flash of insight, would try to forget the kiss, deny the significance of it. She accepted that—for now. He was accustomed to being on his own and would no doubt fight against what was happening between them. She'd bide her time. She came from stubborn stock.

It was odd, she thought, the way he filled places in her heart that she hadn't even known were empty.

Nick stood, needing to put some distance between them. Every instinct urged him to draw her into the circle of his arms once more, to hold her and never let her go. When the longing grew too great, he jammed his fists into his pocket. When the sweet smell of her hair drifted up to meet him, he turned his head. When the need to kiss her threatened to overwhelm him, he knew it was time to leave—before he did something they'd both regret. The only problem was, he wasn't sure he'd regret it. That galvanized him to action.

"Are you going to be all right?" he asked.

"I am now."

"Get some sleep." He fitted a finger beneath her chin to tilt her head up. "Promise?"

"Promise."

When he kissed her, her heart hammered painfully. The kiss was as sweet as honey, as soft as a summer rain.

"Thanks," she said again. "For everything."

He kissed her once more before silently closing

the door behind him, the gesture warming her more thoroughly than the desert breeze and sending her heartbeat into a fevered pitch once again.

She wanted to call him back, to tell him she didn't want him to leave, that she wanted to know the sweetness of his lips against hers just once more. She wanted to tell him all that and more. But she couldn't.

She leaned against the door, fingers pressed to her lips as she waited for her pulse to return to normal. A tender smile played across her face as she recalled the way Nick had seen to her needs. No one, outside her family, had ever cared enough for her to put themselves between her and the world. Why this man, at this time?

That was something she'd have to think about.

She admitted what she'd run from for too long. Commitment. Old wariness schooled her against the warming of her heart.

Ever since her fiancé had dumped her, she'd shied away from involvement. Nick was breaching the wall she'd erected around her heart, chipping away at her defenses with slow but sure strokes. She doubted he was even aware of it.

Nick Cassavettes, she thought with a tender smile, was a very different man than she'd first thought. He'd earned her respect and admiration since he'd arrived in town. She was growing uncomfortably aware that he'd earned something else as well. With characteristic resolve, she vowed not to think of it now. She would have no choice once he'd left. And he would leave. She knew he was meant for bigger things. Not because of who he was, but because of *what* he was.

A tiny smile hovered at her lips. Warm and caring, strong, yet gentle. He made her feel cherished. Her smile dimmed as she realized the implications. She was falling in love with him. But was love enough to bridge the differences between them?

His insistence upon staying with her when Lucy had colic, his concern for the people on the reservation, all added up to a man who cared about others. He'd deny it, of course.

How had she not understood it before? Nick Cassavettes, with all his city ways, was what she had been searching for her entire life.

That part of her which was already in love with him needed to believe that he returned her feelings. But how could she know when he kept his own so closely guarded?

She got ready for bed, her heart still heavy with what she'd been forced to do. Sleep persisted in eluding her, and she finally gave it up. But it wasn't only pain that caused her heart to stutter and tremble within her chest. It was the memory of Nick's soothing touch, a touch which had gone straight to her heart.

* * *

After extracting a promise from her that she'd call if she needed him, Nick had left. Slowly, he unfisted his hands from his pockets.

Rachel had been magnificent. She'd done what had to be done with enviable calm. That she hadn't been calm, but torn up inside, only underscored her courage.

He'd almost blown it tonight. What had started as comforting her had nearly turned into something altogether different. If he weren't careful, he'd find himself wanting more from her than friendship, more than help in showing him around.

It was becoming increasingly more difficult to remind himself of the boundaries he'd set for himself. Friendship. That was what they shared. Friendship and a mutual respect.

That was all they could share.

When Jimmy Whitecloud returned from his vision quest, Rachel was chagrined to find herself disappointed. She was glad Jimmy was back. Of course, she was. But his return meant the end of her working with Nick.

The silent admission had her lips turning up. A few weeks ago, she'd had no use for artists in general and one artist in particular. But that had been before she'd gotten to know Nick. Before she'd let him into her life. And, she was afraid, into her heart.

The incident with Snow had made her some enemies among other area ranchers. They stuck by their own. She admired loyalty, but not when it was misplaced. Calls to visit the local ranches and farms had decreased dramatically. If her business dropped off much more, she'd have to cut expenses drastically, maybe even let go one of her employees.

Her lips flattened into a hard line. She'd go without her own salary before she'd do that. Jimmy and Sally weren't just employees, they were friends. And both depended upon the salary, however paltry, she paid.

If she could secure a long-term contract for the state testing, it would go a long way toward giving her business a stable income.

In the meantime, she continued her weekly visits to the reservation. Slowly, the older members of the tribe were beginning to accept her. The younger ones seemed to understand her need to go away for her schooling and greeted her enthusiastically.

She saw Clara Redfeathers watching her. ''Your young man has the look of a warrior about him.'' The old lady gave Rachel a knowing smile.

''He's not—'' Rachel gave up trying to explain her relationship with Nick.

''He has a way with him. He asked me to pose for him. Said my face had character.'' Clara chuckled, the rich sound drawing a smile from Rachel.

Clara Redfeathers was the perfect choice for a model. Her unapologetically lined face and dark eyes held a wealth of wisdom. Her hair, liberally streaked with gray, was pulled back in a braid that reached her waist. Nick hadn't chosen one of the younger, prettier woman. He'd gone for someone whose face reflected years of living and learning. Rachel could only applaud his choice.

She hoped he hadn't offered to pay Clara. Though the old woman had little money, she would resent the suggestion of payment.

"He bought twenty of my necklaces," Clara said proudly. "He told me they'd make wonderful gifts for his friends back in Denver."

Nick had understood that buying jewelry from the old woman would provide her with income while allowing her to keep her pride. A few weeks ago, she wouldn't have credited him with that much insight. She knew differently now.

He was more than she'd imagined him to be. So much more, she now understood. She was thoughtful as she tried to absorb this new aspect of Nick with all the others.

Chapter Eight

When Rachel no longer needed his help, Nick had time on his hands. Too much time. He missed working with the animals, the physical labor, the knowledge that what he did made a difference. Most of all, he missed Rachel.

The end of the job signaled something else as well. He knew he had to face what had brought him to Los Cincos in the first place.

He'd come up with dozens of excuses why he hadn't been painting. He hadn't found the right subject. He didn't have enough time. The excuses were gone and all he had left was the truth. He was afraid.

Nick tacked the pictures he'd taken of Clara Redfeathers to the corner of his easel. Several hours later, he stood back. Her features came to life, a competent enough portrait . . . if competent were all he'd wanted. But he'd failed to capture the strength and integrity, the humor and compassion that were so much a part of her. Had he reached the point where he had to settle for mere competence? If so, it was time to find another career.

Angrily, he tore the canvas from the easel and tossed it aside. Again he tried. And again his efforts came up short. It wasn't the subject.

It was the artist.

He needed Rachel. He didn't bother to question the certainty. Without giving himself time to think better of it, he drove to the clinic.

The familiar smells soothed him. He found Rachel in the back room, cleaning instruments. He contented himself by watching her. When she looked up, the pleasure in her eyes warmed him.

"I missed you." The simple honesty of the statement touched him as nothing else could.

He took her in his arms. For long moments, he held her.

"What's wrong?" she asked when he let her go.
"Nothing."

She didn't buy that. Not for a minute.

He held out a hand. "Will you come with me? I need you."

She didn't have to think about it. She put her hand in his and smiled up at him. The short drive to his studio was made in silence.

Inside the studio, she looked around, searching

for some hint into the nature of the man. There were none, she noted with disappointment. The furnishings were strictly utilitarian, with no stamp of individuality. No family photos were clustered on the mantle, no magazines or mail cluttered the table.

She'd expected something different from an artist, especially an artist of Nick's stature. Boring. It was as though he had deliberately omitted any clues as to his life. The idea intrigued her. Had he kept all parts of his former life stored away in the boxes stacked in the corner? Maybe the past was too painful for him to bring it into his new life.

And maybe her imagination was running away with her.

"Not much to look at, is there?" he asked.

"Why is that?"

He gestured to the pile of taped boxes. "I put the past where it belongs. I'm thinking of putting the rest in there too." He gestured to the stacks of canvases, the tubes of paint.

"But you're an artist."

"I was."

The choice of tense wasn't lost on her. She noticed the canvases propped against the wall. She longed to look at them. Instead, she was afforded only a cursory view of the one on top. She saw splashes of color, bold and brash. It appeared to be unfinished. Several easels held other canvases, each in the same state. Streaks of color, but no form. It was as if he had started painting after painting, only to discard them.

"You're wondering why I haven't finished anything." He didn't make a question out of it and she didn't treat it as such.

"Why haven't you?"

"I can't." The two words, stark and bleak, slapped her. "Sorry."

"Can you tell me about it?"

"I lost my talent the same day I killed my brother."

If she'd been shocked before, it was nothing compared to the feelings she was experiencing now. She searched his face, looking for some clue to what he was thinking, feeling. His expression gave nothing away.

"You can't just leave it like that." She flushed at the accusing tone of her voice.

"No. I guess I can't." He stared past her, as though seeing into the past.

Once more she was reminded of her impression that Nick had ghosts to lay to rest. It appeared now that the ghost had a name. His brother's name.

"Sam lived to take risks. It took more and more to give him the same rush. A couple of times I talked him down from doing something foolish."

"And others?"

"I went along with him. Tried to keep him from breaking his neck."

"You looked out for him."

"I tried. He wanted to tackle a mountain in Wyoming. I promised to go with him. Then my agent wrangled me a showing in this San Francisco gallery. I'd been waiting my whole life for a break like that. It came on the same weekend.

"I told Sam I'd go with him the next time. When I got back, there was a message waiting for me. From the police."

She was looking at him, but she was also looking *into* him in a way she couldn't explain. Instinctively, she knew he needed the sound of her voice. It didn't matter what she said. He needed an anchor to hold him steady in a world that had spun off its axis. She started talking, quiet words intended to soothe. She talked about work, the people on the reservation, Charlie's courtship of Sally.

Her voice, low and musical, worked its own special magic, and he let it spread its warmth over him. He hadn't realized how edgy he'd been until he felt the tension melt away under the soft cadence of her tones.

But his mind wasn't on what she was saying. It was on the lady herself. The realization made his mouth curl wryly. He'd vowed to lose himself in his art and all he could think about was this woman.

The homey chatter stopped, and her gaze found his. "How old was Sam?"

"Twenty-nine."

"Old enough to make his own decisions."

"He should have been," Nick agreed. For the first time he smiled. "Sam was always the wild one, ready to try something new, something different."

Torn between convincing and comforting, she laid her hand on his cheek. "What happened to your brother wasn't your fault. Wasn't anyone's fault."

"I wasn't there. I should have been."

"You tried to talk him out of going."

"I didn't do a very good job, did I?" The drawl in his voice failed to mask the pain in his eyes.

She cared for him too much to see him wallow in the mire of self-pity. "We can't always comfort ourselves with blame."

"Is that what you think I'm doing?" Masculine outrage rimmed his tone. "Comforting myself?"

"It's easier to blame yourself than to admit that there was nothing you could have done to save him. It's a kind of arrogance to think you could have prevented what happened, to assume responsibility for what you couldn't control."

"He was there because of me."

"Sam was there because he chose to be." Rachel said the words slowly, carefully, letting them sink in. "In the end, we're all responsible for ourselves." When he would have protested, she held up a hand. "Don't worry. You can still have your hair coat. But what happened to Sam wasn't your fault."

She'd made him angry, she knew. He'd expected sympathy, perhaps a few tears on her part. And she'd challenged those feelings. She hadn't given him what he'd been accustomed to, and now he didn't know how to react.

"If you'd stop being so self-centered, you'd see that I'm right." Impatience colored her voice.

"Self-centered?"

"Believing that you can control everything that happens to people is a kind of conceit."

"I don't—"

"Don't you?"

That stopped him. "Okay. So maybe I like to be in control."

She raised a brow. "Just maybe?"

A half smile touched his mouth. "Don't push it." The smile faded. "Sam looked up to me. Counted on me."

"If the positions were reversed, would Sam blame you?"

Nick didn't have to think about it. Sam had too much simple goodness in him to bear a grudge. Why hadn't Nick seen that? And why had it taken an outsider to recognize what he should have already known?

"When are you going to start living and stop using guilt as a way to avoid life?"

"You're way off base, lady."

"Am I?"

He scowled, his thoughts churning. Rachel couldn't be right. He wasn't so egocentric as to believe he had to be in control of everything and everyone, was he? Only a fool thought he could control the world.

Yet hadn't he blamed himself for Sam's death?

She gestured to the stack of half-finished paintings. "You say you can't paint because of what happened to Sam. I think it's a lot more simple than that. You're afraid. Afraid that the hotshot artist doesn't have what it takes any more. So you hide behind a wall of guilt."

"Thanks for the sympathy."

The sarcasm nipped at her, but she didn't back down. "I . . . I care about you. I don't like watching you throw away your talent." She hardened her voice. And her heart to what she was about to say. "Now, if you'll take me home, I have work to do."

The harsh words mocked what they'd shared over the last weeks. She ached to erase the grief from his face, his heart.

He gave a curt nod. Rachel realized she'd been holding her breath and forced herself to draw a gulp of air. Her world finally righted itself, and she flushed at the extent of her feelings for this man who had come to mean everything to her.

Nick hadn't liked the home truths Rachel had thrown his way. He felt like he'd taken a blow to the gut. Her unflinching honesty didn't allow for any self-pity. Nor did it make room for excuses. After he'd gotten over his anger, he'd realized she was right.

He remembered how she had looked as she stood there in his studio, eyes blazing, chin jutting forward. She'd shot from the hip, letting him have it with both barrels. He didn't know many men who could or would face him down that way.

He didn't go out for the next two days, but spent time in the studio, brooding and wondering if he had the courage to take up the challenge she'd thrown at him.

The half-finished portrait beckoned to him. He wandered over to the easel.

He'd prove that Rachel was wrong.

A week later, he admitted Rachel had been right. Once he acknowledged his feelings about Sam, he could pick up a brush without seeing his brother's face. His painting was back on track. The art which he'd thought was lost to him forever was coming back. Perhaps it had never gone, but was only hidden inside himself. The theory intrigued him, but not so much that he could stop working.

Clara Redfeathers's face slowly appeared on the canvas. The strong features, unapologetically wrinkled face, gray hair—he put them all in with no attempt to pretty them up. Clara needed no enhancement. Her face was a history of eighty-plus years of living.

A cautious optimism filled him as he worked.

The fear was still there. He wondered if it would always be present. He couldn't worry over that now. For the first time in over a year, he was painting something he believed in. Or maybe, for the first time, he believed in himself.

He worked late into the night, grabbing a bag of chips for dinner and washing it down with a can of warm soda. He barely noticed.

By morning, he had worked nineteen hours straight. The portrait still needed work. He would finish it, then start another. And another. Elation spurred him to call Rachel. He wanted to share it with her.

When, Nick wondered, had he gotten to the point where he needed to see Rachel, if only for a moment, to make his day complete? He didn't bother to worry over it now. The urgency to see her had him taking the stairs to her loft two at a time and rapping on the door.

Logic eluded him when it came to sorting out his feelings for her. If it had been only physical attraction, he could have understood. Rachel was the most beautiful woman he'd ever encountered. But the physical attraction he experienced was only a part of what he felt. And he had no idea how he was going to deal with the rest of it.

First he had an apology to make.

The wariness in Rachel's eyes when she opened

the door caused his lips to twist wryly. Well, what did he expect? He'd all but snarled at her the last time he'd seen her.

"Last week, when I took you to the studio . . . I was hurting and took it out on you. I wasn't ready to admit that you were right."

"Was I?"

"Yeah. I've been running from the past for more than a year."

She thought she understood what the admission had cost him. A man like Nick wouldn't be comfortable showing vulnerability.

"You didn't make it easy on me," he said ruefully.

"Did you want me to?"

"What I want is to kiss you."

She raised her lips to his and found there the same overwhelming emotion that she had experienced before and gave herself up to the delicious feel of his mouth. His kiss threatened to dissolve all rational thought.

She needed time to think. And that was impossible while she remained in the warm circle of Nick's arms.

When she flattened her hands against his chest, he released her, although reluctantly. She didn't try to hide the trembling that his kiss had produced.

"I've started painting again. A portrait."

"Clara Redfeathers?"

He nodded. "Thanks to you."

She had news of her own to share. "I got a three-year contract from the state to do the testing."

He picked her up and swung her around. Breathless, she clung to him when he set her down once more.

"Tomorrow night we're going to dinner, then dancing," he said. "We're celebrating."

"Celebrating?"

"Your contract." He kissed her again. "And the rebirth of my career."

She didn't pretend to sleep that night, only closed her eyes and thought about the upcoming date. There was no pretending this time. It was an honest-to-goodness date with the man she loved. And maybe, just maybe, he'd discover that he loved her too.

Reality set in. It was only dinner, she cautioned herself, sharing a meal. Nothing to set her heart racing with hope. And longing. Still . . .

Night gave way to dawn. And still she lay there, content with her thoughts. And dreams. It might not be smart or logical to love Nick Cassavettes, but love him she did. If she could find a way to reach his heart, she'd take it.

"I do love him," she whispered wonderingly. That was it, her secret. The one she'd kept hidden from everyone. Including herself.

No, that wasn't quite true. Sally had known. Perhaps it took someone already in love to recognize the signs.

"I love Nick Cassavettes." There, she had said it aloud. Again. She knew now that she loved him with all her being. Whatever happened between them, she would never again be the same woman she had been just a few short weeks ago. She was playing with fire, giving her heart to a man who might one day give it back.

She thought of what had brought him to Los Cincos. She'd never wish on him the pain that he'd endured, but she was fiercely glad they'd found each other.

The hours dragged by. Rachel caught herself watching the clock, praying for the end of the day. She'd never been a clock-watcher before. Now she resented every hour that kept her away from Nick. At closing hours, she all but raced from the clinic and hurried to the loft to get ready.

The magic took an extra spin when Nick knocked on the door. With hands suddenly gone damp, she opened the door.

"You're beautiful."

The words were quietly spoken, but they sent a shaft of pleasure arrowing through her heart.

"I thought you promised me dinner," she reminded him when he continued to stare at her.

He sighed. "You're right. Mundane things like eating seem to slip my mind when I'm with you."

Rachel couldn't suppress the shiver of delight that his words produced. He made her aware of herself as a woman in a way she'd never been before.

The evening was touched with the kind of fantasy she thought was found only in fairy tales.

The food was tastefully prepared, the background music soft, the man across the table a perfect companion. Funny and charming, witty and insightful. They fit together, she thought.

"Dance with me," he said softly.

She nodded, unable to trust her lips to form the proper words.

He helped her from her chair and led her to the minuscule dance floor, his hand warm on the small of her back.

She came willingly. So very willingly. The flutter of his breath across her cheek was a gentle caress.

They danced, soft curves to hard muscles, velvet skin to lightly stubbled jaw. No words were needed; none were spoken. His hand splayed across her back.

She wondered if he knew of her love for him. The thought caused the color to creep up her cheeks. She lifted her gaze. Even if he was aware of her blush, he could not possibly know the reason behind it.

Or could he?

His hand crept infinitesimally upward until his fingers came in contact with the sensitive skin of her upper arms. She shivered tremulously at his touch and felt butterflies in her stomach. He could not possibly be unaware of her reaction but he gave no notice of it, except to tighten his hold of her ever so slightly.

The words of the old country-western ballad spoke of lovers parting. *Is that what the future holds for us?* she wondered with a pang.

She arched against him more closely, as though she could keep out the rest of the world. For the space of the dance, she succeeded. There was only the two of them. Her head resting in the slight curve of his shoulder, she was aware of only him and the electricity humming between them.

When the music lapsed into silence, Rachel hardly noticed, so caught up had she been in the sensations of being in Nick's arms.

After leaving a tip, he placed her wrap lightly about her shoulders and guided her through the throng of diners. A full moon rode high in the sky, its glow only slightly diminished by a mist of clouds. He steered her toward the car.

Nick slanted a look at Rachel. The muted light inside the truck only hinted at the beauty that never failed to take his breath away. Over the past weeks, he'd learned that that outward beauty was but a small part of her. Her generosity of spirit and indomitable courage continued to awe him as did the sweet vulnerability she tried so hard to hide.

On impulse, he took the long way home, winding through the narrow roads that led through the foothills. He didn't want the evening to end. The soft sighs that spilled from her lips were as evocative as the music they'd danced to a short time earlier.

At the clinic, he helped her from the truck and held her for a moment before setting her on the ground. With his arm around her waist, he walked her to the loft.

The protectiveness he'd experienced upon taking her in his arms was nothing compared to what he felt upon seeing her look up at him with her heart in her eyes. The unguarded expression shook him to the core. He had known, or should have, that a woman like Rachel would give herself totally, holding nothing back. And in doing so, she had entrusted him with her heart.

How had he allowed that to happen?

But when she lifted her face for a kiss, he was powerless to resist her. His lips found hers. The kiss was a symphony of emotions, like Rachel herself. Warm and gentle, tender and giving. She tasted sweet, incredibly sweet.

He gave.

He took.

And shuddered from the intensity of it all.

Sanity and reason returned slowly. What was he doing, kissing her like there was no tomorrow? This was crazy. He shouldn't touch her, shouldn't want her, shouldn't need her.

But he did.

"There's so much we can do together," she said. She whirled away from him, a blur of motion and color. Her energy, her enthusiasm, as always, took his breath away. "Who'd have thought when we first met, that we'd become an *us*?"

"Rachel . . . you matter to me." He took her hand and brought it to his lips.

She was soaring too high to notice the wary expression in his eyes. "You love me."

When he didn't confirm the statement, she looked up at him, a slight smile on her lips. "It's all right to say the words," she said gently. "They don't hurt." Her smile widened. "Not much."

To her surprise, he didn't return the smile. Or the words. She told herself it was because he was reserved, because he thought through every feeling before voicing it aloud. She told herself all that and more.

"I love you." Her voice was level, but her insides were churning. *Let him say the words I want so much to hear,* she silently prayed. He didn't say anything, and a shiver raced up her spine.

She looked up at him, hope plain in her eyes. Her expectant smile made his stomach knot like a pretzel. This was what he'd feared, what he'd dreaded.

Love shone from her, bright and shiny and impossible to deny.

His own eyes stung with unshed tears. It should have been so easy to take her in his arms and hold her close as he had only moments ago. It should have been easy. And it was. Too easy. It was what he wanted, what he wanted more than he could remember wanting anything. And because it was, he couldn't do it.

He'd intended to stay detached. Had tried to. Tried and failed. Bit by bit, he'd allowed himself to fall under the spell of love she wove.

"There's so much we can do together." She looped her arms around his waist.

"There isn't any us," he said quietly, hating himself for saying the words, hating her for making him say them.

She only stared at him, as though his words hadn't penetrated.

With more strength than he believed he possessed, he pulled away from her, trying to ignore the hurt that flared in her eyes.

"Don't." The single word flayed his already raw emotions. "Don't push me away." The plea in her voice almost caused him to relent. *Almost*.

"We can't."

"Can't what? Can't want each other? Can't need each other? Can't love each other?" Curbed frustration marked her voice, frustration he had put there.

He gave a jerky nod.

"Why not?"

"I'm just starting to paint again," he said. "It's all I've ever wanted. It's what I worked my whole life for."

Her brow wrinkled. "Why should that keep us apart?"

"I can't afford to get involved with a woman. Not now."

"Involved? Is that what we are? *Involved?*"

"You're a special woman, Rachel. You deserve better than a burned-out artist."

"You just said you had started to paint again." It was starting to make sense, she thought. It wasn't his art that was keeping them apart. It was Sam. "This is because of Sam, isn't it?"

"Because of what I *did* to Sam."

"You gave him a home, took care of him. In the end, you had to let him go."

She made it sound so simple, and he wished with all his heart that he could believe her. The gleam of moisture in her eyes caused him a sharp tug of regret. And shame. He'd used her. Taken the light and life she offered and used it to reclaim the talent that had once been his.

"It doesn't change what happened," he said. "Or now. Pretty soon I'll be going back to Denver."

"I love you." The stark words, thrown as a gauntlet, challenged him, taunted him, warmed him. It was the latter that was the hardest to resist.

That couldn't matter. He couldn't *let* it matter.

He had no choice. He had to make his stand now. Or lose the very essence of himself. He was drowning in his feelings for her. "Don't you understand? I can't marry you. I can't marry anyone."

The light went out of her eyes. And his heart.

"Why don't you yell at me? Call me a couple of the names that I deserve." He'd have preferred that to the stark pain in her eyes.

"If it'd help, I would. I'd yell at you, call you every name in the book. But it won't change things, will it?"

He didn't answer. He didn't have to.

"I thought we'd been through this. You weren't to blame for Sam's death. It was a horrible accident. I can't imagine what you went through. But it doesn't mean you have to punish yourself for the rest of your life."

What was she trying to do? Offer him absolution?

If that was what Rachel had in mind, she was wrong. He'd cost Sam his life with his tunnel vision, his self-absorption. If he'd been more sensitive, less selfish, maybe his brother would be alive today. If . . .

How he hated that word.

He'd come to grips with Sam's death. But that didn't leave him blameless.

He stared at Rachel. How could he leave this woman? How could he not?

"I love you," she said simply. She wanted to shout the words. To tell him everything inside her heart, the way she was alive only with him. But he didn't want to hear that, didn't want to hear anything that might tie his life with that of another. How had she not realized that before?

She had, she realized in a burst of honesty. She'd known and she'd ignored it, hoping, praying she could make him leave the past behind and take what the present offered, what *she* offered. He'd rejected not only her, but a future as well.

Chapter Nine

The following morning she felt as though her heart was shriveling in her chest. She swallowed back a sob. There'd be time enough for tears later. Right now, she had work to do. The animals she cared for didn't care that her heart was breaking.

She went through the motions of work, her hands sure and competent. But her mind . . . and her heart . . . were with Nick. Always Nick.

He was a good man, a strong one.

What he didn't realize was that strength didn't have to stand alone. If only he could accept that admitting need—in particular, needing *her*—didn't translate into weakness. Needing, wanting were all part of loving.

For ten years she had focused her energy toward one end. Earning her DVM and setting up her own practice. Nothing had been allowed to interfere with it. When the other girls had been giggling over boys and buying prom dresses, she'd had her nose buried in a book. When her roommates attended football games, she'd worked in the college dorm cleaning bathrooms and serving food.

She'd worked like a demon, going to school full time and working to support herself. She hadn't minded the eighteen-hour days or the near poverty she'd lived in. She was weaving the pattern for her life.

Her grandmother had woven blankets, her nimble fingers creating intricate designs. Instinctively, she'd known what colors to use, what warp and woof would achieve the most beautiful motif. With quiet patience she had passed her art down to Rachel, sharing her talent and love for the tradition with her granddaughter. Rachel had eagerly embraced it, finding the thousand-year-old art satisfying in a way she hadn't expected.

She rarely had time to practice the skill now, but she hadn't forgotten the peace it provided, the reassuring sense of continuity. She liked to compare the patterns she wove with the patterns of life. Cycles, repeating with the occasional variation, appeared if you looked hard enough. She'd created her own pattern, different from that of her parents and grandparents but rooted in the traditions of her past just the same.

Nick had taken the carefully woven fabric of her

life, and with a few snips at the threads, had unraveled what she'd worked so hard to achieve. She had reached the point where she could admit that nothing would be the same for her when he left. How could it be?

When her parents had died, she'd thought her life had come apart at the seams. Carefully, thread by thread, she'd rewoven it, forming another pattern, different but just as strong. Now she had to make yet another change, insert a different color into the complicated pattern she called life.

She'd fallen in love with him. What she did with that was up to her.

Tears spilled over and ran unheeded down her cheeks. For once, she allowed herself the luxury of crying. She cried for herself, for Nick, and for what might have been.

Wryly, she acknowledged that she had been—was—so in love with him that she could barely think straight. *"When it happens to you, it'll hit hard,"* her grandfather had told her. As usual, he had been right.

The night stretched long and empty before her.

A night's sleep did little to banish her heartache. She had dragged herself from bed at 6:00. A careful application of makeup failed to disguise the circles under her eyes, and she gave it up in disgust.

Sally must have guessed that something more than the pressures of work were troubling Rachel, but she was too tactful to say anything. Instead, she handed her a cup of coffee.

"It's fresh," Sally said with her easy smile. "Made it only three days ago."

In spite of the pain that wrenched Rachel's heart, Sally's smile pulled an answering one from her. She took a sip of coffee and decided Sally was exaggerating. "I've decided all men are stupid and totally unnecessary."

Sally gave her boss a knowing look. "You're in love with him."

Rachel's smile turned wry. "How'd you guess?"

"It's only the people we love who can make us furious."

Sally's logic was irrefutable, Rachel decided. If she didn't love Nick so much, she wouldn't be so angry at him. She released a feathery laugh that sounded dangerously close to a sob.

"In answer to your next question, no, he doesn't love me back. He's not interested in me, much less a family, and he was very sorry he didn't make it clear in the first place before I was fool enough to fall in love with him."

"He called you a fool?"

"Not in so many words." No, it had been worse than that. He'd apologized. Told her it was his fault and that he accepted the entire blame.

What woman wanted to be apologized to after she'd declared her love to a man?

Sally wrapped her arms around Rachel and rocked her back and forth. "He's a jerk."

"Yes." That wasn't right. Nick was a good man. "No."

"Make up your mind. You can't have it both ways. Either the man's a jerk or he's not."

Rachel recognized what her friend was trying to do and was grateful for it. She tried another smile. Her effort must have fallen flat, for Sally frowned.

"Jerk or not, you love him."

Direct hit, Rachel thought. She loved him. That wasn't going to change, however much she might want to talk herself out of it. And the truth was she didn't want to stop loving him. Loving Nick had enriched her life. She wouldn't trade the last weeks for anything.

"When you want to talk, I'm here," her friend said quietly.

Rachel was grateful for the quiet understanding.

The day dragged with irritating slowness. At each ring of the phone, she snatched up the receiver and hoped to hear Nick's voice, praying he'd changed his mind.

It never came.

As the hours wore on, she began to accept the fact that she wouldn't hear from him today. Might not ever hear from him again.

She was in love with Nick Cassavettes. Irrevocably, utterly, in love with him. How had it happened so quickly? Yet love wasn't measured by the calendar or the clock. It came quietly, stealing up on one with a fine disregard for days on the calendar.

She'd given him everything—her heart and soul, mind and spirit. Was the point of giving the very essence of herself to someone who didn't want it, who had tossed it right back at her? It was downright discouraging.

In her loft, after assuring Sally that she'd be all right, she shed her clothes and collapsed on her bed. To her surprise, sleep came immediately. Forgetfulness did not come with the release of sleep, though, for her dreams were punctuated with memories of Nick. Nick teasing her, Nick kissing her, Nick holding her as if he would never let her go.

Mercifully, the night passed without any calls, but the uninterrupted sleep had done little to restore her spirits. A cup of coffee might jump-start her sagging energy. The jolt of caffeine revived her body but could not ease the throbbing ache that pinched at her heart. Only time could do that.

She hoped.

The hoped-for ease never came.

Get over it, girl, she chastised herself. She was a grown woman who had known her share of grief. Losing Nick was not the first sorrow she'd ever experienced. It probably wouldn't be the last.

That wasn't right. You couldn't lose what you'd never had. And, despite what they'd had together, Nick had never shared the essence of himself with her. Her beliefs precluded physical intimacy before marriage, but what she'd needed from Nick was something even more precious—emotional intimacy. Except for that one notable time when he'd been vulnerable as he'd told her about his brother's death, he'd denied her that.

She wanted nothing more than to crawl back to bed and bawl her eyes out. Her shoulders straightened. She refused to give way to the misery. If she did, she might never find her way out of it.

A weak light filtered through the room's one tiny window, sending fingers of pale sunshine across the walls. She watched the play of shadows, fascinated by the subtle shifts in color and patterns. Early morning had long been a favorite time of day for her, a time for reflection and thought. Now, though, it seemed unbearably lonely.

She gulped down a cup of coffee, scalding her tongue in the process. *Great,* she thought. *Nothing like a second-degree burn to shake you out of self-pity.* Carefully, she set the cup down. Her hands were shaking so badly that she could barely hold it.

She stalked to the closet and yanked on her clothes. She'd spent enough time wallowing in a mire of self-pity.

The unexpected cloudiness that greeted her as she

stepped out the door echoed her mood. She welcomed the leaden sky. Perhaps the grayness of the day would mask the pain in her eyes, a pain makeup had failed to cover.

Sheer will carried her through the days. It didn't ease the pain in her heart, but she managed to perform her duties without breaking down in tears. It had kept her going when she worked eight hours a day and carried a full load at the university. It would serve her well again. In a few weeks she'd be able to deal with it. *Sure you will,* she thought.

Getting Nick out of her mind was proving next to impossible. She threw herself into her work. Fortunately, reports to the department of animal control demanded her full concentration. Guiltily, she realized she'd left too much of the paperwork to Sally.

Heartache was no excuse for neglecting her work. And she had mooned about for too long. With a vengeance, she threw herself into the work, finding a numbing relief in entering columns of numbers into tiny blanks of closely spaced rows.

After an hour of filling in reports, Rachel leaned back in her chair and reached around to gently knead the tensed-up muscles in her shoulders and neck. She was unable to reach the area that most needed attention and found herself wishing that Nick was here. He would know how to relieve the pain. Ironically, she thought, if Nick were here, she probably wouldn't even notice the tension.

A call from Ben Winslow had her practically running out of the office. Give her a cow with mastitis any day over paperwork. Mud and muck were preferable to the morass of filling out reports.

Back at her desk, she viewed the reports with distaste. With a feeling akin to martyrdom, she tackled them again. Slowly, the pile in the IN basket diminished while the OUT basket filled with completed and signed forms.

At the loft, she went through the mechanics of preparing dinner—salad and a soda. After pushing around the same piece of lettuce for the last twenty minutes, she admitted defeat and shoved the food down the disposal.

Hearts do not really break, Rachel decided as she got ready for bed. *They may bruise. Or crack. But they don't break.* She was living proof of it. If her heart was really broken, she wouldn't be able to feel.

Right now, she felt too much. All of it pain. Hurt, sharp and ragged, scraped at her as she remembered Nick's reaction and she wondered how she could have totally misread his feelings.

To her surprise, sleep came quickly so that she didn't notice the tear-dampened pillow beneath her cheek.

The old saying, "out of sight, out of mind" didn't apply, Nick decided after a week of misery.

He slammed a fist into his palm and groaned aloud the name that had haunted him throughout the long days and the even longer nights. ''Rachel,'' he whispered. ''Rachel.''

Memories taunted him as he recalled the sweetness of her lips, the softness of her voice.

She filled his thoughts, and his dreams. And he wondered how he'd ever thought he could get through the days without her.

Rachel was out of his life, but not out of his mind. Or his heart. He suspected she was there to stay. And, somehow, he would have to learn to live with what he'd done to her . . . and to himself.

He ached to go to her, to take her in his arms and hold her. Even as he thought of her, he knew he couldn't.

He hadn't been able to pull himself from the blue funk he'd fallen into. He was having difficulty concentrating. His attention, as ephemeral as a desert mirage, kept drifting away. His eyes kept straying to the clock as he wondered what Rachel was doing.

A glance in the mirror confirmed how he felt. Lines furrowed his forehead and fanned out from the corners of his eyes. Eyes that were bloodshot with worry and gritty with fatigue stared back at him. He showered, pulled on fresh clothes, looked at his reflection again, and scowled.

He yanked his latest canvas from the easel and tossed it to the floor. His work, which he'd believed was finally back on track, had disintegrated in the last week until he barely recognized it as his own. The brushstrokes wobbled pitifully, the normally confident lines now hesitant, weak, and indecisive.

Fred bounded to him. With a resigned sigh, Nick submitted to having his face washed with a rough, pink tongue before picking himself up and brushing dog hairs off his shirt.

He recalled how Rachel had looked, brow furrowed in concentration, as she tended Fred's wounds. She gave every animal she treated the same attention, gently caring for their injuries. Nurturing them. Loving them. Just as she did with the people she surrounded herself with.

For a moment . . . only a moment . . . he indulged in a fantasy of Rachel and him together, married. The fantasy dissolved as reality hit him. What did he know about commitment? Or permanency? Or loving and cherishing a woman?

Nothing.

He wasn't the right man for her. Someday, she'd understand and appreciate the fact that he'd had the good sense to get out of her life before he destroyed the love she'd offered him. She'd get over him and find someone who'd love her as she deserved to be loved. A mirthless smile tightened his lips. Probably a lot sooner than he liked to contemplate. She was too lovely, too full of life to stay alone for long.

She'd find someone else. Someone who could

give her everything she deserved. Someone who wasn't scarred by the past . . . someone who knew how to love.

If he were any kind of a man, he'd be happy for her when it happened. And he would be, he promised himself fiercely. Even if it killed him.

He pictured Rachel repeating the sacred vows of marriage, a beaded ceremonial dress highlighting the creaminess of her skin, the dark sheen of her hair. The image was so vivid, so intense that he had to shake his head to dispel it.

The loft which Rachel had taken such joy in decorating held no comfort. It was empty and lonely and sad. Not since her parents' death had she felt so totally alone.

She'd taken to spending evenings outside. Twilight had deepened, the hazy clouds of late afternoon chased away by the purpled shades of evening. Shadows dimpled the ground, their shapes ever shifting, phantoms of the night.

She lifted her head, wanting to catch a bit of breeze. The dry air brushed her skin, but it held no hint of coolness. Even the land, which she loved, failed to bring her pleasure.

A movement in the shadows caused her to look up.

"Rachel." Nick's voice, as deep as the velvet night, reached her.

For a moment, she knew a quick surge of hope. It died just as quickly as she realized he hadn't come because he'd changed his mind. Her eyes adjusted to the darkness. A fresh wave of longing washed over her at his nearness, and she gripped the edge of the porch for support. She schooled her voice to an expressionless tone. "What do you want?"

His voice matched her own. "We need to talk."

"I thought we'd said everything there was to say."

Something flickered in his eyes. Pain? She wasn't given a chance to wonder about it as he carefully banked any further expression.

He held out a hand, the gesture one of entreaty that tugged at her heart. "We're still friends. Right?"

Friends? That was a poor substitute for what she wanted with him. Despite everything, she loved the man. Loved the sensitivity he tried so hard to hide. Loved the gentleness he showed to people and animals alike.

Some of what she felt must have shown in her eyes for he closed the distance between them in one long stride.

He cupped her shoulders, bringing her close enough that she could smell the scent of him—turpentine mixed with musk aftershave. She inhaled deeply and knew this scent would be forever imprinted in her memory.

"Rachel . . . I never meant to hurt you."

She wanted to laugh. And cry. Of course he hadn't meant to hurt her. Somehow that made it worse. She found the courage to push away from him. It cost her everything she had, and she trembled with the effort. "I know."

"I'm sorry." The two words hung between them until he turned and left.

She went back inside and tried to still the pounding of her heart. The small measure of peace she'd achieved over the last few days had crumbled under Nick's touch. How was she supposed to get through the rest of the day, much less the rest of her life without him? For, despite everything, she loved him.

She faced the rest of the night with resignation. There was no hope for sleep.

She arrived at work an hour early, intending to catch up with her reading. She picked up the latest journal on animal husbandry with a sense of martyrdom.

When the front door opened an hour later, she realized she'd spent over an hour reading the same page. She composed her face into what she hoped was a normal expression and walked out to the office.

"What's wrong?" Sally asked after taking one look at Rachel's face.

"Nothing."

Her friend raised her eyebrows at Rachel's uncharacteristically short tone but said nothing.

Rachel's smile came and went. "I'm sorry. I didn't mean to bite your head off."

"It's all right. Sometimes love stinks."

"And sometimes it's beautiful," Rachel said softly, thinking of what her parents had shared.

Sally twisted a long strand of hair around her finger. "I wanted to wait, what with you feeling so down and all, but Charlie wants to tell everyone and I told him you have to be first to know."

Rachel's brows pinched together as she tried to follow the convoluted sentence. "First to know what?"

"Charlie's asked me to marry him." A pretty blush stained Sally's pretty face.

Of course. If Rachel hadn't been so caught up in her own problems, she'd have seen the signs.

"I'm so happy for you." She gave her friend a quick hug.

"I hoped you'd feel that way."

"Why wouldn't I . . ." Realization came, and with it, a flash of guilt. "I've been pretty wrapped up in myself lately, haven't I?"

"Just a bit." Her friend's smile softened the gentle rebuke.

"I'm sorry."

"You're hurting. And heartache's the worst kind of hurt there is."

Rachel blinked back tears at the gentle understanding in the words.

Tears formed in Sally's eyes as well. "Look at us. Tears falling faster than a waterfall."

Rachel was proud she could give her friend a genuine smile. "No more tears," she promised. "Except happy ones."

Sally's face was flushed with happiness. "Charlie got a job with the park service. With me working for you, we think we can swing a house pretty soon. It won't be much, but it'll be ours."

"I wish I could afford to pay you more . . ."

"Hey. I wasn't complaining."

"I know." Still, she wished she could raise Sally's salary. It was almost impossible for a young couple just starting out these days to afford a home of their own. Though they could live with Sally's parents, she knew Charlie would never agree to such an arrangement. She approved his choice— newlyweds needed time to get to know each other without the onlooking of overly concerned parents.

They spent the next hour making plans. Her earlier sadness melted away as she rejoiced in her friend's happiness, and her bruised heart felt better than it had since Nick had told her good-bye.

Rachel pressed a kiss to Sally's cheek. "I'm so happy for you. You and Charlie."

"Thanks. I didn't know . . ."

"Hey, we're friends. Friends want what's best for each other, right?"

"Right." Sally looked at her in concern. "What about you?" she asked gently. "What's best for you?"

Nick. The answer came immediately.

"Are you gonna be all right?" Sally asked.

"No," Rachel said honestly. "But I will be." *In time,* she added to herself. *Lots of time.*

Stop it, she told herself. *It's for the best.* Try as she would, though, she doubted she'd ever convince herself of that.

Rachel was strong, Nick thought, much stronger than he was. She could and would survive without him, but he was far less sure that he could say the same for himself.

He accepted the blame for the disastrous meeting. He'd gone there to find peace, not for Rachel, but for himself. Telling himself that it was for her benefit. A lie if there ever was one. He'd wanted, needed, to see her once more. His selfishness had only made it worse. For both of them.

Touching her had been a mistake. He'd wanted to see her again, listen to the sweet cadence of her voice, hold her. In a moment of weakness, he'd indulged himself.

The peace he sought wouldn't be found that way. Peace, real peace, would be found only in himself.

Chapter Ten

Rachel made the mistake of looking in the mirror. And nearly gasped at the hollow-eyed stranger who stared back at her. She knew she'd been pushing herself the last week. Working until her body begged for rest, cleaning the barn until the stalls were sterile, and spending the dark hours of the night pretending to sleep.

She shrugged philosophically. Her looks had never mattered overmuch. What mattered were the neat stack of bills ready to be mailed. For once, her practice was well into the black. Why wasn't she happier about it?

Her eyes felt hot and itchy, and a lump grew in the back of her throat to match the heaviness that settled around her heart.

Nick.

She'd like to assign him to a distant planet, preferably somewhere outside the galaxy. That he refused to stay there only kindled her anger further. Only she wasn't sure to whom it was directed—herself or him.

The pain had mercifully blunted to a dull ache. It didn't rip her apart as she'd feared it might. She needed to eat. Most of all, she needed Nick. She needed him to love her as she loved him. She needed his arms around her, his lips upon hers, his strong presence.

She managed to summon enough energy to eat breakfast. She picked at the toast and eggs she'd forced herself to make with little enthusiasm. They tasted as flat as she felt.

Resolutely, she started eating. One bite at a time, she reminded herself. One step at a time. One day at a time.

It wasn't that she'd buried herself in work; it was that work buried her. A horse that had torn up its leg on barbwire. A cow with mastitis. A dog, a family pet, which had been bitten by a coyote, and the owners feared rabies. Each took time. Each took energy. She was grateful she had both to give; even more so, she was grateful they forced her mind away from her own problems.

She pushed her way through the day by sheer force of will. And if she gave way to the heartache that was never far away, no one knew. What had seemed so important weeks, even days, ago had faded into insignificance compared to what she had lost.

Nick. And a chance at a lifetime with him. By the end of the day, she could swear she heard her feet crying. Nineteen hours without a break.

Nick had filled the empty places in her life, places she hadn't even known existed . . . until he'd shown her. A soft warmth stole over her as she remembered the tenderness of his kisses.

He was good for her in so many ways. When she started taking herself too seriously, he teased her out of it. When she needed someone to talk to, he was there. When she rushed in to solve problems, he reminded her to take things one step at a time.

Couldn't he sense, couldn't he feel how much she loved him? How dare he say he wasn't the right man for her? He was the man she'd been waiting for all her life, the only man she'd ever wanted to spend the rest of her life with, the only man she'd ever uttered words of love to.

A heavy feeling filled her. *Love.*

But the sweetness she wanted to feel was tainted by barbed edges, as sharp as the wire that fenced off the county. Foolishly, she'd believed that love was unblemished. She knew differently now.

Like a movie slowly flickering to life, her memory stirred, and image upon image appeared. The gentleness of his hands when they framed her face.

The strength of his arms when he held her. The warmth of his lips pressed against her own.

Other memories came rushing back as well, scraping at her heart. She didn't want to remember how safe she felt with him, how protected and cherished he made her feel just by holding her. Giving into the memories, she sighed, frustration mingling with wistfulness.

When had she fallen in love with him? Had it been the first time he'd kissed her? Or maybe it had happened when he'd comforted her during the long vigil over Lucy. Was that all she was to have of him, she wondered with piercing heartache, pictures tucked away in her mind?

Impatient with her musings, she closed her eyes, willing the memories away. It didn't matter when it had happened. Or how. Or why. Life had played a cruel trick on her by allowing her to fall in love with the right man who believed he was all wrong for her.

If only . . .

She shook her head. Wishing was futile. More than that, it was dangerous. It encouraged you to think about the might-have-beens. Her breath caught in a tiny sob. Might-have-beens had no place in her life.

Perseverance, hard work, and sheer will had gotten her through school when all the odds were against her. But she feared determination alone wasn't enough to convince Nick that they belonged together.

Grandfather Ray wouldn't have much sympathy for her head-in-the-sand attitude, she thought. He believed in meeting life head on. "Troubles grow smaller when met with one's eyes open," he was fond of saying.

When he showed up at the clinic the next day, she wasn't surprised. Somehow, he always knew when she needed him. Still, she didn't feel like telling him what a mess she'd made of her life and lowered her gaze.

He didn't press her for information, didn't ask useless questions, but opened his arms.

Without hesitation, she walked into them and laid her head on his shoulder. He didn't utter any platitudes or give false reassurances. Instead, he simply held her. She felt his quiet strength seep into her, filling her with peace.

"Thank you," she said, lifting her head. "You always know what I need." Her grandfather went off by himself several times a year "to cleanse body and soul." He had powers few understood. Though she was among those who didn't fully understand, she respected him. She had witnessed the wisdom of his ways too many times in the past to doubt it.

"I had a vision."

The words brought a faint smile to her lips. Perhaps Grandfather Ray had seen what she needed to do to put her life back in order.

"I saw a hawk."

Her smile faded. The hawk carried bad connotations. "Did you see anything else?"

"It hovered above a dove. Then it disappeared. In its place was an eagle."

Though she didn't understand all the meanings attached to vision symbols, she gave a small sigh of relief. Eagles were good omens.

Her grandfather's eyes were filled with love. "You must look within yourself and see where the fault lies."

"But . . ." Her protest fell away. Hadn't she tried to tell Nick how to live his life?

He looked at her with his too-shrewd eyes. "Your heart is in pain."

She could only nod. She had never been able to hide her feelings from him.

Grandfather Ray took her hand in his and turned it palm up. He stared at it for long moments, and she wondered what he saw there.

"Things do not happen without a reason, granddaughter. The man had a purpose in coming here, and someone has a lesson to learn from it."

"That someone being me?"

His eyes were unreadable. "That is for you to know."

But I don't know, she wanted to shout. It seemed

she didn't know anything anymore. Except that she loved Nick.

"You will find the way, if your heart is open."

Despite her heartache, she smiled at the familiar words of advice. Her grandfather never changed. For that, and so many other things, she was grateful.

He brewed tea.

As she sipped the chicory and bitterroot, she remembered another pot of tea, shared with Nick. Then it was she who was offering comfort.

By the end of the week, she told herself she was feeling better. She repeated the words over and over, as if sheer repetition could make them true. The memories haunted her a little less frequently. The pain was a little less intense. And the honest corner of her brain called her a liar.

The truth was she was miserable. It had been the longest week Rachel could ever remember living through. If you could call this living, she thought wryly. All the joy had vanished from her world and, for the first time in her life, she dreaded getting up and facing each new day. Not even the intense grief she had experienced after her parents' death equaled the heartache she was experiencing now.

The way she had succumbed to Nick's kiss at their last meeting was a constant rebuke to her. Even knowing that he didn't return her feelings, she still wanted him . . . still loved him.

Images of him flickered through her mind. His

patience during the long vigil over Lucy. The sense of humor that surfaced at odd moments. She feared she would always judge other men by him. And she was very much afraid that none would measure up. Nick's failing was only in refusing to see himself for what he was—a caring, decent man.

Her parents, and then her grandfather, had brought her up to have confidence in herself, in her abilities. The independence they had instilled in her had served her well. Until now.

She functioned automatically, going to work, home, and back to work again. Knowing that Sally would welcome the extra time with Charlie, Rachel told her assistant that she'd take over the evening shift of manning the phones. If she couldn't be with the man she loved, she might as well make it possible for Sally to be with Charlie.

Nick made no more attempts to get in touch with her. She was grateful for that. The sooner she put him out of her mind, the better. Sometimes, at work, she was able to actually succeed and, for a short while, she was almost her old self again. But eventually the memories returned, and with them, an anguish that tore at her heart.

The nights when the phone remained stubbornly silent, when the long hours stretched endlessly, were the worst of all. Then, she imagined Nick's arms about her, his lips touching hers. She relived every moment that they had spent together, savoring each precious memory and storing them up to take out and replay when the pain grew too bad. Even the knowledge that she was only driving the knife deeper into her heart failed to stop her tormented thoughts.

Sleep did not come easily, when it came at all. And then it was punctuated with dreams of Nick.

People noticed. How could they not? Her ready smile and quick laugh were conspicuous by their absence. Her skin lost its luster, and she grew noticeably thinner. Her belt was notched on the very last hook, and still her clothes hung loosely on her. She knew that Sally was worried about her and made an effort to throw off her depression when she was with her friend.

Gossip about her and Nick spread hot and furious through the town and reservation. She was too weary to resent it.

"What's going on between you and Nick?" Darlajean Thompson asked as she refilled Rachel's coffee cup as she sat slumped in a booth at the diner.

Rachel had ordered a piece of Darlajean's pecan pie and was trying to get it down. Even that failed to tempt her appetite. She tried hard to work her lips into a smile. It felt like a lie. "Nothing." That, at least, was the truth. Nothing was going on between them now. Or ever again.

The snatched looks in her direction showed curiosity, but the warmth and concern behind them robbed them of any offense.

"Word around town was that you and that painter feller were gonna make a match of it," the sheriff put in from the booth adjacent to hers.

"Make a mighty handsome couple," Darlajean added. Her pretty face screwed up into thoughtful lines. "Though you look lower than a snake's belly in a wagon rut."

Rachel looked at her two friends in exasperation and affection, knowing their meddling was prompted by genuine feeling.

"She looks like something the coyotes ate," Wally Simmons added his two cents worth.

She grimaced at the description. "I'm fine." The lie was so plainly obvious that she felt her cheeks blaze with color. "Okay, so I'm not fine. Satisfied?" Immediately, she regretted her show of temper. "I'm sorry." She pulled some bills from her purse, slapped them on the table, and fled.

It was the same at the res when she showed up for her weekly visit.

Clara Redfeathers, still quietly proud that she'd been chosen for a portrait, took Rachel aside and studied her, her old eyes missing nothing. "The painter. He is not with you?"

Rachel shook her head.

"You have displeased him."

Clara believed that a woman's duty was to please her man. Rachel had different ideas, but she knew better than to argue with the old woman and the traditions of thousands of years.

She wanted to shout that *he* had displeased her with his refusal to give them and their love a chance. Instead, she pressed Clara's hand. "He knows his own mind."

Clara looked at her wisely. "A man who fights himself has already lost the battle. Give him time. He will find the words when the time is right. Until then, you must have faith."

Rachel appreciated the comforting words, but she wondered how much truth there was to them. Nick had had no trouble in finding the words to tell her that she had no place in his life.

Nick was bone-weary, his muscles crying out for mercy. The gas gauge nudging empty, he drove into a gas station. Thirty more miles, he thought, as he pressed the pedal, and he'd be home. The word gave him pause. Since when had he started thinking of Los Cincos as home?

He bought a sandwich he didn't want from a vending machine and choked down a bite of stale bread and turkey. In disgust, he threw the rest away.

It had been a grinding three days of driving and then arguing with his agent. He'd opted to drive

Desert Paintbox

rather than fly. The long hours concentrating on the road were preferable to the tormented thoughts that filled his mind.

And then there was Fred. He couldn't very well leave the dog alone. Nor could he ask Rachel to take care of him. So he'd brought along a supply of dog biscuits and prayed that Fred didn't get carsick.

Fred had handled the trip with aplomb, even behaving himself while Nick met with Jerry. Jerry had taken one look at the ugly mutt and shook his head.

Jerry hadn't minced his words when it came to the few pieces Nick had brought with him. "Competent enough. We can probably sell them."

What was the saying about faint praise, Nick thought, recalling his own disgust with the idea that he might merely be competent.

Jerry looked at his friend, his eyes filled with pity. Pity, Nick discovered, was worse than anger. "You're a fraud. You say you can't paint because of guilt. The reason is you're afraid. You're running away from Sam's memory."

Nick had bristled at that. Hadn't he pulled himself and his brother out of poverty? Hadn't he fought his way into a profession that routinely chewed people up and spit them out?

Twelve hours later, Jerry's words still stung. Nick scowled at the memory. And at the truth behind them. He had never run from anything in his life, but he was running now. Running from his art. From his agent. From Rachel.

Rachel. The hitch at his heart was a quiet presence. It tugged at him, at times, twisting his heart inside out.

The ribbon of road unfurled before him. He longed for the quiet of Los Cincos. With any luck, he'd make it by nightfall.

As he pulled into the drive of his studio, he waited for the feeling of homecoming. All he felt was emptiness. At Fred's insistent bark, Nick opened the truck door for him. Fred watered the shrubbery.

Nick let himself inside. Wandered through the place that had become home. Restless, he opened the French doors and stepped outside. Stars blanketed the sky, diamond chips draped against black velvet. Night sounds, the cry of a coyote, the screech of some small animal filled the night.

He thought of Rachel. Strange how everything reminded him of Rachel these days. Maybe not so strange, he silently amended. She was a part of him whether he wanted to admit it or not. He had a feeling she always would be. He imagined he could fear her pulse beating alongside his own.

She was so much a part of him that whatever he saw or thought or felt—the morning's sun on his face, the colors of the desert sky at dusk, the shrill

Desert Paintbox 173

howl of a coyote—his own reaction was heightened by picturing how Rachel would react and a longing to share it with her.

She had been right about a lot of things. Including his guilt over Sam's death. Without ever having met Sam, she knew he wouldn't want his big brother blaming himself for his death. She had an instinct for people, an intuitive sense about what they wanted, what they needed. She'd given meaning to his life when he believed he'd lost everything. And he had turned her away out of fear. Disgust rolled through him as he wandered back inside.

He picked up a brush, toying with it, wondering if he would ever again use it as it had been intended.

It felt good in his hand. Right. He took a couple of imaginary strokes. On a whim, he set up the easel. Tonight, he would let the fear go and embrace the simple joy of creating.

The first hours, he didn't try to paint. He played. Color. Texture. Form. Each was a part of the whole. He splattered the paint, flicking it from the brush, giving a stippled effect. He felt like a child with his first set of fingerpaints.

Inevitably, his thoughts turned to Rachel. The stunning beauty that could knock a man flat at ten paces. The courage, spirit, and fire that turned beauty into something rare and precious.

Inspiration came, a blinding light that demanded immediate attention. He stripped off his shirt and went to work. Stroke by stroke, her features came to life, the strong brow, the stubborn chin, the high cheekbones. Fourteen hours later, he stood back and stared at the canvas. Bold streaks of color defined a traditional squash blossom design. At its center was the woman who was life and light to him.

The talent he'd once thought lost to him forever was there, in his hands, his mind, his heart.

He worked quickly, his hands sure and confident as he sketched in her face.

A grin, his first in the last couple of weeks, stole across his lips. She'd made him take a good, long look at himself, whether he'd wanted to or not. What he'd seen wasn't particularly pleasant.

Needing a break, he stepped outside, surprised to find the sun high in the sky. The midday sun nearly blinded him. It was savage, this heat. It was also healing. He stood there, heedless of the sweat that trickled down his neck to run in rivulets down his chest.

It wasn't totally quiet. The comings and goings of a town at work made that impossible, but there was a harmony to it, a quiet meshing of lives and jobs. He had missed this in the few days he'd been away, the serenity that even the newfound prosperity of the town couldn't erase.

It felt good to be home. His use of the word startled him. Since when had he started thinking of Los Cincos as home?

Desert Paintbox 175

For most of his adult life, he'd lived in a city where the hustle and bustle had continued to grow along with his dissatisfaction with it. Denver was a great city, as diverse as the people who made their homes there. But he no longer thought of it as home.

He didn't want to live in Denver anymore. He realized something else. He didn't have to. He could paint anywhere. It surprised him, the sudden certainty of his decision. It felt good.

Three hours later, he stood back to look at the canvas mounted on the easel.

The painting was the best work he'd ever done. He knew it. There was no arrogance in the feeling. Or even pride. Only simple truth. When he called his agent with the news, Jerry was ecstatic.

"I'll be there. If it's as good as you say, we'll contact the press, hold a special showing."

Nick took a deep breath. Even knowing Jerry's tendency to go overboard, he hadn't expected this big of a reaction. What if he'd been fooling himself? What if the work wasn't as good as he thought? He felt compelled to add a warning. "Jerry, you haven't even seen it."

"If you say it's great, that's all I need to hear. All you needed was to get over that guilt you kept heaping on yourself. Was I right?"

And the right inspiration. Rachel.

"I'll get a flight for tomorrow. Don't bother picking me up. I'll rent a car." Jerry hung up before

Nick had a chance to tell him the painting wasn't for sale.

Suddenly hungry, Nick headed to the refrigerator. He grimaced, remembering he hadn't done any shopping in over a week. Unless the contents of his refrigerator had miraculously changed, he had little hope of finding anything.

In addition to forgetting to eat, he'd also neglected to shower. He stepped into the shower stall with its ancient plumbing. The hot water and steam drew out the tension of fourteen hours straight work. He closed his eyes, letting the spray pummel his neck and shoulders. His hunger forgotten, he fell into bed.

After a full night's sleep, he felt better than he had in weeks. By the time Jerry arrived, Nick's euphoria over the painting had faded to be replaced by gnawing doubt. What if he'd only been fooling himself? What if the painting were only mediocre, like everything else he'd managed to finish over the last year?

When Jerry showed up, he didn't bother with a greeting but demanded to see the painting. He was silent for so long that Nick feared his friend hated the work. When Jerry did speak, it wasn't what Nick expected. "Who is she?"

What was Rachel? The woman who'd brought his talent back to life. The woman he'd learned to love.

The woman who loved him. "A friend," he said at last.

Jerry gave a low whistle. "Some friend." He continued to stare at the easel.

"Is it any good?" Nick asked. Impatience gave an edge to his words.

"You don't need me to tell you. You said it yourself. It's the best work you've ever done. And it's opened a whole new direction for you." Jerry rubbed his hands together. "I'll start the publicity right away. First major work of renowned artist after more than a year. Influence of the Southwest. You know the drill."

"It's not for sale."

Jerry stared at him incredulously. "You're kidding, right?"

"No."

The one word, as stark as the desert after a windstorm, had Jerry raising his brow. He looked like he wanted to argue, and Nick prepared for a fight.

Jerry had a stubborn streak as long as a summer drought. That was part of what made him such a good agent. It might also break up their friendship. He looked from Nick to the portrait and then back to Nick. "I hope she's worth it."

Nick didn't pretend not to understand. "She is."

"Okay." Jerry's capitulation made Nick wary. "On one stipulation. You do another." He held up a hand when Nick would have protested. "Not the same woman. I'm talking style. Feeling. Passion. Bring all that to your next work and make it quick. I can't hold off on something like this forever."

Nick let out a long breath he hadn't realized he was holding. "Thanks."

Jerry left soon after that, but not before extracting a promise from Nick that he'd start working immediately. "You're going to be the critics' darling," Jerry had said.

Nick realized he didn't want to be anyone's darling but Rachel's.

He was in love with her.

He didn't recoil from the thought as he once might have. He simply accepted it. She was a part of him just as he was of her. He wanted a lifetime with her, for only she could look at him the way she did, as though she could see the feelings inside him that he hadn't dared to explore yet. He wanted that more than he could remember wanting anything . . . or anyone.

He pushed back his chair and stood, smiling for the second time that day.

He would go to her, ask her to forgive him. It would take every ounce of courage he could muster to face her. He'd have to find that . . . somewhere, but he'd dig deep inside himself until he did. And while he was at it, he'd ask her to marry him. If he were going to make a fool out of himself, he might as well go all the way.

He *had* been a fool. He'd been prepared to turn away the love of a good woman because of fear. Sure, he had lots of noble reasons why he couldn't marry Rachel. Reasons like he didn't deserve her, didn't deserve to be happy. Reasons like she'd be better off with someone else, someone who wasn't flawed. The truth was he was running scared.

In the safe cocoon he'd created for himself over the last year, he'd shut himself off from pain. He'd also shut out love.

Rachel Small Deer was the best thing that had ever happened to him. She'd restored his belief in himself. Why had he failed to understand that before? He'd find the words to tell her how he felt. His future depended upon finding a way to convince her that he loved her, that he'd spend the rest of his life proving it to her.

Rachel surveyed the loft. It had never looked better. She had washed windows, polished furniture, scrubbed floors, even cleaned the oven—a job she detested, but she'd tackled it, trying to stay ahead of the memories that wouldn't leave her alone. If she ran hard enough, fast enough, then maybe, just maybe, she wouldn't have time to remember . . . to feel . . . to want.

Her strategy wasn't working, she acknowledged as she crawled into bed. Her body screamed against the workout she'd forced upon it, crying for sleep. But her mind was achingly alert. As was her heart. She didn't need sleep; she needed Nick.

After checking her calendar the following morning and finding it clear for two hours, she did what she did so often when her heart and mind were troubled; she drove to the mountains. She navigated the coiling road with practiced ease. When she reached a clearing, she stopped the truck and climbed out. The view stretched before her, a panorama of unequaled beauty.

Rachel never came here without feeling transported back in time. That had always been the appeal for her, to escape to a time when none of her problems existed. The scenery, magnificent though it was, was secondary.

Still, she spared a glance for it. Gorges, deep and forbidding, carved the land. In the distance, the town lay, a speck compared to the vastness of the desert. Ribbons of wind fluttered around her, causing her to shiver slightly in her cotton shirt.

Mountains poked their crowns through low-slung clouds. The clouds themselves were candy cotton puffs against the New Mexico blue sky. Sunshine filtered through them, dappling the ground in a crazy quilt of shadow and light. The land worked its healing magic on her as it always did, pulling

Desert Paintbox 181

her into another world, tempting her to leave her heartache behind. She gave herself up to the quiet and let the wind and heat cleanse her mind in a way she could not.

An hour later, she drove home, her heart more at peace than it had been in weeks.

Nick headed to the clinic. When Sally met him with fire in her eyes and outrage in her voice, he tried to defend himself, giving up only when he realized that her anger was fueled by her friendship with Rachel.

He let her get it all out before explaining why he'd come.

Her fury faded to be replaced by a speculative look. "How do I know you won't hurt her again?"

"Because I love her."

She nodded shortly. "Good."

"Where is she?"

Sally jerked her thumb to the barn. "She took a drive. When she got back, she headed to the barn. She's been spending a lot of time with the animals. Seems to prefer them to some people I could name."

He winced. "I get the message." Guided by the sound of the soft murmur of Rachel's voice, he walked to the far end of the barn.

She heard him first. The steady, sure footsteps could be only one man. Slowly, she stood and turned to face him. She ignored her fluttery heartbeat and concentrated on his face. It was all she could do not to fling herself in his arms then and there. But she waited, hoping.

The long look he gave her missed nothing. She'd lost weight. Her skin was paler than usual. But her eyes were steady.

"Don't," she said as he reached for her. "Don't touch me."

She looked suddenly delicate so that he did as she asked and didn't touch her. He feared if he did, she might break in his hands.

With an effort, he kept his hands at his sides. "I needed to see you."

"Why?" The bald question had a smile nudging at his lips. She didn't waste time with niceties, he thought.

"I was a fool." He said the words flatly, with no apology or excuse for himself.

She nodded.

"An idiot."

That got another nod from her.

"A jerk."

He grimaced. "Are you just going to sit there and nod?"

"I was waiting for the rest of the apology."

"You want an apology? Okay, here goes. You were right. All along. I was just too darned stubborn to admit it."

Her lips twitched at the admission. "So what took you so long to tell me?"

He gave her a rueful look even as a matching smile pulled at the corners of his mouth. "Pride."

She muttered something uncomplimentary about male pride and earned another smile from him.

His smile slipped a notch. "I'm sorry for what I put us through." His eyes turned dark. "I need you, Rachel. And I'll always love you. Whatever else happens, that's not going to change."

Slivers of lovely anticipation assailed her senses at the promise in his voice. He wrapped his arms around her, hauling her against him. This time, she went willingly. His mouth opened and covered hers.

The grayness of the last weeks vanished as she came alive under his touch.

He let go of her to drop to one knee. "Rachel Small Deer, marry me. Please." He reached into his jacket pocket and produced a small jeweler's box. Opening it, he said, "I should have waited, let you pick out your own ring. But I saw this and . . ." His voice trailed off, but not before she heard the hint of nerves.

That small thing gave her confidence. She'd love the ring, whatever it was . . . because it came from him.

He stood, took her left hand, and slipped the most beautiful ring she'd ever seen onto her fourth finger. Turquoise nuggets nestled together on an intricately carved silver band. It was traditional and yet totally unique.

She stared at her hand clasped in his. Both were strong, yet each was different. As they were. When, at last, she looked up, she said simply, "I love you." The words slipped out, as easy as a breath, as natural as a sigh.

A relieved sigh shuddered from him. Only then did she notice the package at his side. Heavy brown paper covered it. She looked at him questioningly.

"I have something to show you." He pulled a penknife from his pocket and slit the paper. After hesitating a moment, he held an unframed canvas up for her view.

She simply stared. It was her. But it wasn't. The face that looked back at her glowed with inner joy, the eyes soft and luminous, the lips full and slightly parted. "Do I really look like that?"

The love in his eyes was answer enough. "I told my agent it wasn't for sale."

"You're keeping it?" She hardly dared hope. Even to her untrained eye, she could see that it was an important work, possibly the most important he'd ever done.

"*We're* keeping it. Someday, we'll point to it and tell our children and our grandchildren how you brought me back to life."

"All I did was love you." It was as simple as that.